TIME MACHINE EMERGENCY

DAN ARTHUR BUSBY

CHAPTER ONE

Derek rolled over in bed and slapped that nagging alarm clock. All was finally quiet, and he began fading away again, but caught himself just in time.

He sat up at the bedside, rubbing his eyes, and disbelieving the quick passage of time since getting off work at 11pm. Professor Kibble was driving a hard bargain at the university. He was currently running an experiment trying to change the molecular structure of honey. The purpose was to thin it into something "with more marketable properties". He was demanding all hands on deck to finish what he thought would be a huge money-maker.

Derek thought about his work in Kibble's lab. Sure, it was fascinating, but starting to get pretty demanding. He was presently not taking any classes, trying to save for next year's tuition.

According to professor Kibble, he was a "kid genius", though he was 22. At work he was delegated lengthy math problems and chemical experiments. Derek snorted while reaching for his clothes. If he was that valuable, why didn't Kibble sponsor his education. He could definitely afford it.

That morning at the lab, professor Kibble was all wound up. At first sight of him, Derek knew it was going to be a slam-bang kind of a day. "Glad you're here on time, Derek, my boy!" he seemed genuinely enthused. "Today we might get the break we've been looking for!"

Derek loved how Kibble always talked about "we" when he really was excluding himself. "Here we are", Kibble went on. This is the centrifuge, and it's going to redistribute the honey molecules into a delectable taste and texture that will go over big!"

Derek stopped and stared at a table upon which sat a machine looking something like a space capsule. His mouth dropped open as he did a double take at the professor. "Uh...what am I going to be doing here?"

Kibble jumped right in as if on cue. "It's going to be simple, Derek. The honey will be in a closed container in the center. It will be spun as fast as anything known to man. You know the drill. Test it at different speeds, and keep track of the empirical data."

The professor shuffled off, and Derek followed. It wasn't long before they had loaded the honey and buckled everything down tight. They spent the morning running the spinner at different speeds. The machine had controls for temperature, humidity, and even pressure.

Derek and Kibble both were impressed by the flavors and textures that resulted, but something else caught Derek's eye, and he said nothing about it. During high spins the canister of honey would become weightless, floating up into mid air inside the shell. During these occurrences, the digital clock on the side of the canister actually moved backward in time.

Derek went home to his small apartment, and could think of little else than this amazing discovery he had made. He would have to get to the bottom of this somehow.

Professor Kibble's honey experiment worked out well, and he started doing the marketing end of things. Derek was able to procure the 'space capsule' machine, since Kibble was using different equipment. The thing barely fit through the door of his apartment. He became obsessed with studying and experimenting during his spare time.

Weeks flew by, and Derek was making some astounding discoveries. He'd come upon evidence that objects placed in the spinner really were falling back in time. He could make adjustments to carry the items further back. The more speed developed by the spinner, the further back in time it went.

He had sent it back as far as several hours.

Concrete ideas developed in his mind to bring the scale up in size and power.

Over the next several months Derek worked feverishly, and saved money to buy materials for the upgrade. He seriously thought about talking to the professor, mostly for financial reasons. Finally, he made the decision that it was necessary for professor Kibble to be involved.

One day before going home, he found himself in Kibble's office. He stood inside the door, just about ready to knock, when the professor's eye caught him.

"Well, Derek, you look as though something is on your mind. Come out with it! Just what is it?"

Clearing his throat nervously, Derek looked at the professor and began to speak.

"There's something you must know about". He started to speak again, then hesitated, shook his head, and pursed his lips. "I'm just going to tell you straight. It's something very important that I need your help with".

Kibble's thick eyebrows narrowed. "Sounds big, Derek. What is it?"

"OK", Derek shuffled his feet. "I really always thought that time travel was impossible." He looked squarely at the professor. "Now I'm not so sure."

A befuddled look covered Kibble's face, and his lower jaw sagged. He'd had enough experience with Derek to know that whatever he said was usually right.

"It's the spinner, Professor. There's something about speed and weightlessness that causes time to backtrack in that environment."

Kibble had regained some composure. "I assume you've done some testing on this."

"A bunch." Derek was emphatic. "I know that whatever you put in that spinner is not in the same time zone as the rest of the world. It's older".

Professor Kibble dropped his head and twisted his mustache, deep in thought. He looked up at Derek and spoke convincingly. "This is between you and me...no one else."

He stood up behind his desk and began nodding. "We have a lot of testing to do, young man. Let's get started."

The two scientists went at it in earnest the very next day. Little did they know that world events were shaping into a crisis that would push them up against a deadline.

CHAPTER TWO

The year was 2026, and the once wide-spread freedom in the science world was closing up. Any research project was required to be approved by a federal board. This severely limited creative experimentation, such as this that had fallen into the hands of Derek and Professor Kibble.

Hence, the strict secrecy of the project.

To complicate matters, global strife was increasing. The Chinese and Russians were both expanding their borders, and not responding to sanctions or threats. Europe was in a state of disunity and economic weakness. This left it up to the US and a few allies to keep the balance of power at an even keel.

There was an air of tension exceeding that which prevailed during the cold war. In fact, a feeling of doom lurked in every corner of the free world. All that could be done was to sit back and watch the globe crumble under totalitarian rule.

Professor Kibble decided the project should be kept in his garage. Business at the lab should be carried on as usual.

The plan was to build a large scale capsule...big enough for a man to enter, and which could be moved in and out of a garage. Derek actually spent most of his time in the garage, while the professor carried on at the university. He consulted after hours and on weekends.

Kibble once came home after a day's work, finding Derek grinning from ear to ear. "I've got something to show you." He blurted out. "Sit here and watch." He then placed a large rubber ball in the center of the capsule, and walked out, latching the door behind him. He flipped some switches, which started the machine humming and spinning. The two men sat idly for a few minutes until the noise suddenly stopped.

Derek opened the door, holding out one hand, palm up.

The professor peered in and saw it...nothing. The ball was gone! "Blazes!" Shouted Kibble. "You've done it! But the question is, how far back did it go?"

Derek squinted at the gauges on the inside wall. "Ten years, not a day sooner. I programmed it to bring the spinner back. But if someone is seated inside..." He frowned and scratched his head. "We have to program the entire capsule to travel in order to return."

"How close are you with that technology?" The professor stood, hands on hips.

Derek shook his head. "I'm in sort of a quandary there."

Kibble slapped the capsule wall with one hand. "Say no more. I have a theory, and I'll bet you it works. You've already done the hard part. We'll start tomorrow."

"Works for me," Derek grinned, "but how are you going to swing your schedule?"

"I'm on sabbatical starting tomorrow. If we can't do this in a year, it can't be done."

Kibble wasted no time getting under way. He knew where to pick up parts and tools for the project. He and Derek did multiple tests, and went over two different theories before settling on one...the correct one.

The theory stemmed from this: after they understood what happened with the honey experiment, they should be able to do the same thing on a larger scale. The main difference would be two seats in the spinner, and a tough exterior for protection.

The professor's idea bore fruit right away. After a few weeks of study, testing, and construction, the whole thing began to shape up.

Professor Kibble decided that they were going to need a secretary/aid/housekeeper to keep them from getting bogged down in mundane chores. He did some interviews and came up with someone he thought could do the job, and be trusted. Her name was Lex. She was a middle-aged go getter with fiery red hair. She could cook as well, which would help immensely.

Kibble explained to her what the project entailed...and the dangers involved for himself and Derek. But she was just to stay at the home station and serve as a navigator, communicator, or whatever came up.

The two scientists were checking and rechecking systems, tightening bolts, making sure all was in order for the next step.

Derek stood up gripping a wrench, and giving the thumbs up sign. "Everything is functional to the best on my knowledge."

Kibble was putting away tools and plan books. "Yes, but you know we'll never know for sure of anything unless we try it. I think you know the risk. Once someone sits down and pushes the buttons, he's going to disappear. And really, where is he going, and will he return?"

Derek strolled toward the professor, nodding his head. "Sure, we know the risks. We've gone over this before. I'm going to test it first...alone. It's an unknown, but I'm willing to go. There must be a destination, and I will arrive there, hopefully alive. And hopefully, I'll be able to come back."

"I know there's no sense in both of us going," Kibble responded, "when one man can operate the machine easily by himself. It's the danger of losing both of us at once. Such a high risk...and not necessary."

"The other question is this:" Derek spoke slower, and more emphatically. "How far back do we set the maiden voyage? Ten minutes or ten years?"

"Probably ten years." Kibble spoke with no hesitation. "You need to know that it really does work, and get all your questions answered."

"The last question is, when do I sail?"

"Indeed," Kibble said convincingly..."tomorrow."

CHAPTER THREE

Lex was still getting the lay of the land, her 4th day on the job. And this was the very day they were testing their invention, newly coined, the 'Doormac'. Door, meaning the portal back in time. Mac simply short for machine. She could hardly contain herself in the excitement of it all.

Nonetheless, she tried to stay out of the way to avoid becoming a nuisance.

Derek had been studying data from prior tests. Lex was organizing the project papers into a file, and seemed captivated by the doormac. "So what do you think it will be like putting yourself in this machine for the first time?" She sounded entranced. "I mean, aren't you afraid that you'll disappear into oblivion, or slip into some third dimension, and get stuck floating around somewhere?"

He put the papers down and looked at Lex. "The test items really are traveling into the past, but here's the real question. Can a human survive the transition through the threshold of time? It's a scarey thing to attempt, because no one's ever been across that barrier. I don't know what effects it will have on a person."

"You know I'm not trying to plant a seed of fear into you." She apologized. "I'm just asking questions."

"It's OK." Derek laughed. "It's definitely scarey, but I'm definitely still going to go through with it."

Lex rested her hand on Derek's shoulder, and shook her heal. "You're braver than I am."

The time for action had come. All three were gathered at the doormac. Professor Kibble was going over last minute theories and suggestions. Derek had strapped himself into one of the two seats in the spinner.

"Remember." Kibble warned. "If you are in danger of re-materializing into matter, the red light comes on, so push the abort button."

"It's not like I didn't help design this system, Professor."

He ran his fingers along the instrument panel. "I still think I'll be able to maneuver around solid mass. If not, I will abort before it's too late."

He pushed a button and typed on the small keyboard in front of him. "OK, I'm setting this for ten years ago- 2016."

Kibble twirled his mustache, as he always did when he was nervous. "And don't tarry! Just come back as soon as you gather the data you need."

"Check." Derek signaled the thumbs up. "Let's get rolling!"

Kibble gave him a friendly pat on the back, exited and closed the door.

Taking a deep breath and exhaling slowly, Derek placed his thumb over the power switch. He thought for a moment, prayed for a moment, and flipped the switch.

The shell which surrounded the seats, began to spin. He felt vibrations and heard a humming sound. He himself was not spinning, but all around him was ever increasing speed. The whirring around his head got so intense that he lost equilibrium. Soon he could feel the seat floating in mid air, being held by straps.

The vibrating got worse, and the whirring got louder.

He felt as though he were in a speeding train. The speed, the noise, the pressure, all reached a climax...then the sound barrier was broken, as it were. The pressure was released.

The noise and wind leveled off, and finally stopped.

Derek opened his eyes and looked around the interior of the doormac. The instrument panel had powered down. A couple of small cabin lights remained on.

He moved his arms to release the seat belt. Snap...and he was free. Standing up, he put one hand on the door latch and pulled the door open. A chilly night breeze brushed against his face. He saw total darkness. Poking his head out the door, he tried to take in the surroundings.

It appeared to be a driveway in a residential area. His first step felt like pavement. Taking a penlight from his pocket, he scanned the area. A driveway...the doormac had landed in a driveway. Was it the professor's driveway of ten years ago?

Scouting around, he found that, indeed, it was Kibble's place, before the addition was built on. The cars in the neighborhood were ten years older but still appeared new.

Kibble's car must be in the garage.

It suddenly occurred to him that he hadn't known Kibble longer than two years. He would be considered an intruder.

Walking quickly up the driveway, he confirmed the home address, and bee lined back to the doormac. He really had all the information he needed. It was important to get back before being noticed.

Derek secured the door and buckled himself down. Programming the timing for the return trip, he flipped the power switch.

Lex and the professor were dealing with an uneasy stretch of time. In spite of his optimism, Kibble really didn't know whether to expect Derek's return. Or, if he was to return, when it would be. He was scanning a stack of experimental data, while Lex had busied herself with household cleaning.

The whirring came to an end, finally. It seemed to take longer on the return trip. Breathing a sigh of relief, he unbuckled and stood, grabbed the door latch and pulled.

A sudden flash of sunlight, a gust of aroma from a field.

He rubbed his eyes, struggling to see what this was. The doormac was sitting in tall grass, flat terrain. From the left was a distant sound of voices.

Derek felt a chill down his spine. Something had gone terribly awry. The voices came ever closer. He quickly checked coordinates on the screen. "Oh no!" He groaned. He had programmed the return trip for 1,000 years into the past!

As he reached for the door, they came into view...a large company of Indians scampering toward him. They appeared to be carrying battle gear, complete with bows, arrows, and spears.

Derek slammed the door and quickly sat down, frantically programming another trip home...or anywhere!

They were there now, surrounding the doormac. Their voices sounded like they were close enough to be shouting right in his face. The hollering and screaming began. Spears and arrows ricocheted off the outer shell.

His hands trembled as they worked feverishly to finish...the year 2026, May 5, Enter. The humming started, then whirring. His attackers were jostling the outer shell, getting ready to topple it over.

CHAPTER FOUR

"Hurry up...kick in!" Derek stressed out loud.

Boom! Whine! Whirr! Professor Kibble jerked, nearly falling out of his chair. Wide-eyed and grinning from ear to ear, he stood and began pacing, shouting, gesturing the victory sign.

Lex burst through the garage door, joining in the celebration. The noise died down, and the doormac door slowly slid open a crack.

"Derek! You did it! Are you OK?" Kibble shouted.

The door quickly opened wide, revealing a pasty white, trembling Derek. He tried to exit, but tripped and fell forward. The two greeters caught him, carrying him to the couch, where he sat blinking.

The professor squatted down and grabbed Derek's shoulders as if to shake them.

"Derek. I can tell something happened. Tell me what it was!"

Derek leaned back and breathed deeply. He shook his head. "That was way too close for comfort." He looked at Kibble. "I did get to the year 2016. It was dark, but I knew it was the right location. Then I got in too much of a hurry to get back. I programmed the return trip for 1,000 years back instead of 10 forward!"

Kibble couldn't believe his ears. "You actually went back a thousand years?"

Derek nodded. "This time the sun was out, and the natives were on me almost instantly. I'm telling you they were shooting at me, even trying to tip the shell over."

Kibble patted Derek's shoulder. "You're OK, Buddy.

Really sorry about the close call, but I'm glad as heck to see you back here."

He stood up and checked the doormac. He ran his fingers over dents and scrapes from arrows and spears. He turned around, gesturing as he spoke. "Here's the thing.

This has got to be planned better for safety."

He started to speak again, then held up. "That's it!" He pointed skyward. "This machine can be planted in a helicopter! You can transport, and immediately take off if you're in danger."

Derek opened his eyes and nodded, signaling that he was paying attention...sort of. "I could have used that helicopter just a few minutes ago. I think you're onto something."

Kibble stepped closer. "Now Derek, I believe we could include that helicopter in the transport field. What's your take?"

"Yes, I really think that is possible." Derek leaned forward. "I don't want to get caught in a situation like this again. I'm also thinking about carrying weapons."

Over the next few months, the two scientists busied themselves with reconstruction of the doormac to fit in the helicopter already purchased by professor Kibble. They both also attended flight school and training. The chopper was kept in Kibble's warehouse in the back of his property.

Lex became more familiar with the basic science of the new secret discovery. Kibble drafted her, reluctantly, to travel with them on future excursions. There would be a crew of three. The aircraft would be well armed, so as to be able to handle any scenario.

Six months after Derek's near disaster, things were shaping up quite well. The technology of Kibble's idea had been completed.

CHAPTER FIVE

Derek had run some test transports earlier in the day, and gone over some formulas. The helicopter doormac seemed to be dependable. As he sat having a bite of lunch, he was alarmed by the news on TV. Global tension had given way to outright war.

Russia and China had not even slowed their expansionist practices. There seemed to be a pact between them to capture more resources in their quest against the west. The U.S. and Canada were involved militarily, but Europe was still crippled economically, and divided politically. There had already been threats of nuclear war.

He and Lex discussed this matter, and awaited the professor's arrival to go over it with him. As Kibble walked through the warehouse door, he was greeted by Lex and ushered into the kitchen area. Derek finished up the chopper maintenance, and joined the party.

Professor Kibble was seated at the table as Derek came in. "I know all about it." He blurted out. "I've been tracking the news." He tossed a newspaper on the table. The front page was filled with fear and panic. "Sounds like we're heading toward nuclear war."

Derek sat down and glanced at the headlines. "I just wonder what kind of responsibility we have. Is there a chance we can do anything to alter the course of history?"

The professor twirled his mustache. "Indeed there is a chance. But my question is this. Will we have peace instead of destruction? Should we give it a bit more time?"

Derek wagged his head and glanced at Lex. "So what's your take on this?"

"Well," she seemed serious, "if there's any possibility we can fix it to avoid what's happening now, we should do it."

Kibble tapped his fingers on the table. "I've got to do some historical research." He said. "Maybe there are some alterations that we can make to change the balance of power."

Arrangements were made to meet the next morning for discussion. Each was to do what research they could, and bring results to the table.

At 7am the gathering commenced. Each had notes in hand. The general feeling was somber. The war had worsened. The Iranians had joined the circle, and had pledged to destroy the west.

Professor Kibble opened the dialogue as he seated himself. "We don't have much time." He began. "The news is bad, and here in Chicago, we are a nuclear target. Let me just say something." He continued. "Whatever we can do to alter the historical course may be a good thing. But we must do something by no later than tomorrow." He looked at the others. "OK, what have you come up with?"

Lex responded. "There are several times in the last 500 years that we might look at. Some occur during the wars between Britain and France. The point is to unite Europe in order to swing the balance of power."

"Exactly." Derek chimed in. "We could assist Napoleon with his invasion of Russia."

"That's all well and good," Kibble added, "but during that time they did have guns. To really have leverage, we should go back well before the advent of guns."

"You see," he continued, "we are going to have to acquire and ship modern weaponry to a chosen point in history. We'll have to abruptly change the outcome of some war that favorably changes history."

"And by 'favorably'," Derek interrupted, "you mean to strengthen Europe."

Kibble nodded. "Or to weaken the Chinese. But China is so huge, it would be tough to make a significant impact there."

"So at what point," Derek pried, "do we change history, and who do we assist?"

Kibble lay his hands flat on the table. "I'll tell you who it must be. In order to give us the best chance to stabilize society...Alexander the Great."

Silence purged the room. Derek and Lex stared at each other.

"Just think about it." The professor continued. "He had conquered most of the known world by the time he was 32. But that's when he died. Had he survived, his kingdom may have lasted to this day. We need his kingdom to thrive and grow long enough to not be split into three parts when he dies. We need to keep him alive in order to do that."

"Then we'll have to befriend him." Lex added. "We could certainly impress him with the helicopter and weaponry."

"Of course it's dangerous." Kibble went on. "But staying here and doing nothing is much more dangerous."

"We're going to have to tell him the truth." Derek emphasized. "That we are from the future, and are trying to save him and the future world."

"One more thing." Kibble pulled out a piece of paper and handed it to Derek. "He died on June 11, 323 BC. We need to be there in early June...and bring Penicillin just in case. It may cure the fever that would eventually be fatal to him. And I'm in charge of the weapons. I have a source."

Kibble twisted his mustache, then spoke up. "Let's leave this afternoon. "Lex will pack food, Derek will do the mechanical maintenance, and I will bring weaponry."

CHAPTER SIX

By the time the group gathered that afternoon, the general consensus was to leave absolutely as soon as possible. The Iranians had already sent off nukes toward the U.S., which had been intercepted. Return warheads were sent, which had reportedly hit their targets. Widespread panic was everywhere.

The three passengers were boarded and buckled in. All food and weapons were secured inside the large military helicopter.

Coordinates were entered for an area just outside of the palace of Nebuchadnezzar II, in Babylon.

"All set?" Derek shouted, as all had secured their positions.

"Is that programmed for June 5, 323 BC?" Kibble questioned.

"Yes it is, and remember this…" Derek's voice was stern. "If we materialize into a hornet's nest, be prepared to backtrack immediately."

He put his finger on the power switch. "Here we go!" Spinning and whirring commenced above their heads, growing louder and more intense. Lex gritted her teeth and held her head down. The professor nervously stroked his mustache. Derek had been through worse. This system was much improved from the original. A bit of shaking and vibrating went on, then the 'sound barrier' pop, which was really a time barrier.

Everything quickly quieted down. The passengers sat up straight and peered out the chopper's window.

"Derek," the professor broke the silence, "you stay put, and be ready to fly this helicopter. I'm getting out to scout around."

Kibble unstrapped and made his way to the back. He opened up a chest, quickly pulling out 3 automatic weapons, placing 2 next to Derek and Lex. He grasped onto his gun and opened the door.

A heat wave struck, along with extreme bright sunlight. Jumping three feet into a sand dune, he scampered around to the tail of the aircraft and spied all around. There it was, about half a mile behind them...the palace of Nebuchadnezzar. It was a grand and monstrous stone building. On the upper balcony, armed guards could be seen the entire circumference of the palace.

Kibble turned around and backtracked into the chopper. "We've reached our destination." He announced. "Listen carefully. I've got a plan, and it's the only way this is going to work. Today is June 5. If we don't interfere, Alexander the Great will drink himself sick, and then die of a fever on June 11. The party will occur roughly on the 9th of June. So we need to be sure that party never happens."

"OK, but how are we going to execute this plan?" Derek queried.

"We've got to make a big scene." Kibble continued. "These people are superstitious. Let's make them think we are gods...at least at first. We'll fly directly over the palace and perform some miraculous feats, like firing a couple of rockets into a hillside. Then we can land somewhere and hopefully get an audience with the great one."

Lex wiped her forehead. "How did I get into this." She moaned.

Derek picked up his gun. "This is why we're here. Not to kill people, but to change history. I think your plan will work."

Lex piped up. "I really hope one of you can speak Greek."

"Oh yes, fairly well." Kibble seemed confident. "Enough to get by."

"And I studied it in school." Derek added.

"Is there anything else before we fly?" Kibble asked urgently. "We need to get going."

CHAPTER SEVEN

They all strapped in again for the flight, and Derek prepared to start the helicopter. The engine started up easily, and rose off the ground seemingly effortlessly.

Their hearts were in their throats, knowing this was going to be high drama, and not knowing what to expect. But the professor's demeanor was not giving away any fear whatsoever.

Derek elevated quickly, and began the short trip to the palace.

Kibble sat next to Derek for ease of communication. "Just go ahead and hover right above the palace. Let them sweat it out. They've never seen anything like this monster...in fact, that's probably what they'll think it is."

Derek floated along slowly. Below they could see soldiers scurrying about, losing their minds. It seemed their only thoughts were to get as far away from this sky demon as possible. If it weren't so serious, Derek would have laughed at the scene.

"You're doing fine." The professor shouted. "Just don't get in a hurry. We have to make a big impression."

Derek went high over the palace, then floated down again, almost getting within jumping distance of the top of the building.

Soon there was no sign of life on the ground or in the building. After a few seconds, Kibble nudged Derek and pointed to an open area in front of the palace. "Let's land over there and see what happens. Keep your weapons handy."

Lex nervously grasped her gun as the aircraft descended lower and lower. It finally touched ground about 300 feet from the front entry.

No one could be seen in any direction. Kibble grabbed some smoke bombs in case of a sudden ambush. "Go ahead and shut it down, but stay here and be ready to go if necessary."

He squeezed Derek's arm." "If you have to, use the big weapons, but only as an emergency measure."

He opened the door and looked back at Lex. "Stay alert. Protect yourself and the chopper. I'm going to try to get our foot in the door. He stepped out, shut the door, and walked slowly ahead, gun in hand.

The silence was so loud that he could hear every step in the sand. Kibble finally reached the steps to the palace doors, and started up. Still not a soul in sight. Upon arriving at the doors, he stepped into the open space, his right foot touching the marble floor.

A shock rippled through his spine as the huge hall came into view. He saw row upon row of soldiers in perfect formation. But they all were kneeling on one leg, facing him, with helmets in hand.

A hundred things went through his mind. He stood there for a moment, frozen in time. His eyes ran from one side to the other across the auditorium. Peripheral vision caught the figure of a man in the corner standing upright and motionless.

Suddenly he knew he should speak. Shifting to the Greek language, he opened his mouth. "We come in peace. We seek an audience with the Emperor. We would be friends."

The figure in the corner then slowly approached. All the others remained motionless, kneeling. The man drew near and stopped within 10 feet.

With a nod of his head, he spoke, sounding in earnest. "Who are you, sir?"

"Kibble trembled inside, but it did not show. "I am from your future. I would like to be of assistance, but I must speak with Alexander the great emperor."

The man raised his hand as if to silence him. "Before I speak, you must tell me, is that a weapon you carry?"

Kibble put his arm through the strap and slung it over his shoulder. "Yes, this is a weapon, but I will not use it. I wish to be friends."

The man drew closer and made eye contact. His form stood erect, and commanded great authority. Kibble knew who he was immediately.

"I am the one you seek." He volunteered. "I am Alexander."

Kibble swallowed hard and struggled for his next words. "I am with two others." He began. "Another man and a woman. We wish to speak with you about something very important."

Alexander rested his hand on his sword. He paused for a brief moment. "You say you are from the future." His voice sounded diplomatic. "I would like to hear about this. I would like to see this great beast which you ride."

He turned and barked an order. All in the room stood together. He spoke again, and they all dispersed. A small group of soldiers accompanied him as he spoke to the professor. "What is your name, sir?"

"I am Kibble." He bowed slightly. "I will show you the machine called a helicopter." He began walking slowly toward the door. The emperor and soldiers followed.

Down the steps they went, Kibble leading the entourage.

Derek and Lex suddenly perked up, seeing the group heading their way. The professor appeared to have the situation under control, so they opted to stay in their seats, but gripped their weapons.

As the company approached the aircraft, Kibble motioned for them to step out and join them.

As Derek stood, he remarked, "Follow Kibble's example.

Hang the gun strap over your shoulder to appear less threatening."

The two exited the helicopter and slowly walked to the professor. Kibble motioned with one arm. "These are my associates, Derek and Lex."

Lex stood motionless, not comprehending the language being spoken. She and Derek both seemed intimidated by the sight before them...ancient soldiers in full garb, including swords and spears.

At the same time, the emperor seemed even more in awe of the aircraft. He stepped next to it, and raised a hand slowly, wanting to touch, but hesitating.

The professor took the initiative. Opening the door, he asked, "Would you like to see inside?"

Alexander peered into the cockpit, taken in by the utter complexity of this iron beast. He looked at Kibble for a moment, as though he were deep in thought. He then smiled, backing away a couple steps. "This will be later," he stipulated. "Now we will go to the green room. I must know more about you."

CHAPTER EIGHT

Guards were posted around the aircraft, as the party took a stroll along a stone pathway which followed the perimeter of the building. The emperor led, followed by two Generals. The time travelers took the middle, and 6 soldiers brought up the rear.

Lush greenery dominated the edges of the pathway.

The size of the palace was even greater than its appearance at a distance. After several minutes of walking, they turned left onto a smaller path, leading to a fabulous flower garden.

Vines and exotic trees towered overhead, as the floor turned into marble. In the midst of the floor were tables and benches, also made of marble.

Alexander posted the six soldiers at the trail's end. He then motioned to the visitors. "Please, have a seat." He moved and spoke with etiquette well refined.

The professor's group took one side of the table, while the king, and his closest leaders took the other.

"Mr. Kibble," Alexander began, "these are two of my generals; Antigonus and Ptolemy. Please tell us who you are, and why you are here."

The professor lifted his chin slightly. "Gentlemen," he began with utmost confidence. "You have seen how we arrived today. I am here to tell you that we have traveled from the future."

The two generals looked at each other. Alexander stared unflinchingly at Kibble.

He continued, "We are not gods. We are men, as yourselves, except we live 2,349 years in your future."

He didn't hesitate, but went on. "Why are we here?

The real reason is to save our world of the future. But it will also save your own world."

Alexander spoke up. "Tell us, sir, how does our world need saving?"

Kibble found himself twirling his mustache, knowing what he would have to say next. He took a deep breath. "History records you, Alexander the Great, as an unequaled conqueror. However, it also records that 6 days from now you will die."

The emperor gripped the table edges and leaned forward, a confused and angry look on his face. "How should this happen? It is a time of peace."

"Yes," Kibble agreed. "History records that you will perish with a fever. But now I can prevent that from happening. All you need to do is follow my advice. It is easy. Do not engage in excess drinking of wine. It is the cause of your death. So now you do not need to die."

Alexander seemed greatly relieved. He then posed another question. "Tell me, why do you want to help me in this way?"

The professor smiled. "The reason is simple, If you die, your kingdom will be split into many pieces. We need it to stay together and remain strong. That will be good for the future...for our world."

Kibble once again kept speaking. "We have something valuable to offer you. The flying machine that we have has many powerful weapons. It can destroy your enemies from the sky. It also carries many hand weapons like this." He held up his automatic weapon.

Alexander shook his head in disbelief. "I find these stories of yours incredible. If I had not seen your arrival, I would not believe it." He held up his hand and looked at Kibble. "Come, show us how your weapon works. The one you are holding."

He stood up, and everyone followed suit. Kibble and company led the way past the stone trail, and to a grove of trees. He turned the switch to automatic, quickly pointed to the tree tops, and fired. A 20 foot section of branches were blown away. The Greeks stared, mouths gaping open.

Alexander stepped in front of the professor and held his hands out. "I would like to try it." Kibble offered him the gun, explaining a few basic things. Alexander then gripped the weapon and held it up, just as Kibble had done. He pulled the trigger and blasted some branches to pieces.

Suddenly he burst out with hardy laughter. He turned and handed the gun back to the professor. "Kibble," he exclaimed, "if I had these weapons, I would rule the world until I grow old."

Kibble returned a grin and nodded. "That's what we wish for you, and we would like to help you accomplish this."

"Alright," the Emperor agreed. "I have no choice but to believe what you say. We will work together to accomplish both of our goals."

Kibble held out his hand in friendship, and Alexander grabbed it firmly.

CHAPTER NINE

The time travelers were given quarters inside the palace which consisted of a large living area, and three separate bedrooms.

They met with Alexander on a daily basis to formulate plans to spread the kingdom westward, while maintaining good organization everywhere else. Kibble stressed the importance of the conquest of modern day Europe. This consisted of everything north and west of Macedonia. He also advised instituting a finer culture in the north country, thus eliminating Russian expansionism.

Alexander held a keen interest in molding and shaping civilizations for the better. He was developing an even keener fascination for time travel.

The date was now June 12...one day past his historical death. The group was gathering in the green room.

Alexander had developed enough trust in his visitors to attend without his security guards or generals.

Lex had attended all the meetings, not understanding the Greek conversation. She was somewhat frustrated with this, and when Alexander sat at the table, she said "Good morning" in English. The Emperor did a double take at Lex, raising his eyebrows. "And good morning to you." He responded at once.

Lex was taken back. She grinned and shook her head. "Had I known you spoke English, I wouldn't have felt like a castaway all this time."

He burst out with another of his hearty laughs. "As a young man, I studied many languages, and can now speak several. My father, who was king, gave me the most thorough of educations."

Derek and the professor sat at the table, amazed at the genius sitting across from them. "So what do you think?" Kibble inquired in English. "Can you understand me better in English or Greek?"

Alexander chuckled. "It really makes no difference. Your Greek is very good, but I would enjoy conversing with your friends."

Derek chided his agreement. "I do know a few lines of Greek," he smiled, "but I really can't do well with it."

"Sounds like a consensus." Alexander slapped the table lightly. "Now, I'm anxious to get to the topic of the day."

"That would be time travel." Kibble said as he sat up straight. "The fact is, we need to go back to our own time to see if the world has been destroyed. We can also bring more weapons back with us."

"That," Alexander commented, as he thrust his pointing finger into the air, "is where I come in. It is important for me to go to your time, just to experience it briefly."

The professor twisted his mustache in thought. After a moment, his looked up.

"This is what we should do." He began. "Alexander and I will travel to 2026, our own current time, to check out the situation. We will then travel back, carrying a load of weapons. When we return, Lex and Derek will go back and return again."

Preparations were made to make the trip that day.

Word had been sent down the chain of command about the time travelers and their provision of futuristic weaponry.

As the group reached the helicopter, a large portion of the army was lingering to get a glimpse of the excitement.

They knew their commander was scheduled for a trip to the future.

Without hesitation, the professor and Alexander climbed into the cockpit, and buckled in. Coordinates were entered, and the spinner was started. Alexander had been briefed on the routine, but was still not prepared for the experience. As the humming and whirring rose to a fever pitch, he had to grit his teeth and lean his head back to endure the unaccustomed noise and dizzy feeling.

Finally, the loud popping sounded, and the decibels decreased. Alexander felt a great relief. He looked around, half expecting a new scene, but darkness prevailed.

Kibble was there unbuckling himself. He put his hand on the door, and looked at Alexander. "Wait just a moment while I turn on the light."

He navigated the darkness, and flipped the light on, which was a shock to Alexander. Now it could be clearly seen...the familiar confines of the warehouse. Kibble breathed a sigh of relief. He looked at Alexander. "You can get a glimpse of 2026...follow me.

Alexander stepped out of the helicopter, and joined Kibble, who was entering the kitchen. At the TV, he flipped the news on, and immediately saw scenes of cities turned into piles of rubble. Alexander was dumbfounded by this unheard of technology, but Kibble shook his head in dismay. "The destruction has begun. Many great cites are destroyed, and the air is tainted with poison. We must hurry."

He flung the warehouse door open and took it in...eerie pink skies, accompanied by strong wind. An unpleasant odor dominated.

He made eye contact with Alexander, who stood next to him. "Take a look," he said. "It's a dying world."

Pulling the door shut, he headed for the stockpile. "Let's load the weapons and get out of here," he shouted over his shoulder. The men lugged a wooden crate of guns aboard, along with more chopper ammo, plus hand grenades, etc.

As they were strapping in, Kibble sighed. "This is our whole objective... to avoid nuclear warfare. A nuclear weapon will cause wide-spread radiation, which brings on terrible diseases and birth defects. This can take hundreds of years to recover from."

Alexander shook his head. "I am appalled at such a weapon. It should be outlawed."

Kibble nodded. "We will work together to create a more stable world for the present and future."

Programming the trip back, Kibble flipped the switch and started the motion.

CHAPTER TEN

A great cheer went up when the helicopter came into view exactly where it had departed. Alexander stepped out of the cockpit, and motioned for silence. He then told his men that there would be an announcement later today. That would be after the meeting with Kibble and company.

Derek and Lex were dismayed at the news of their lost world. They knew that their relatives would probably not survive the nuclear winter coming.

At the green room the familiar foursome met once again. Faces were somber, as they realized how serious their business was.

Kibble directed the conversation to around the western front...Europe. "In the future, the land to the west of Macedonia will be valuable, and many powerful nations will thrive there." His tone intensified. "Why not bring them all under your control right now, while the taking is relatively easy."

Alexander raised his head, teeth clenched, and a look of resolve on his face. In a move that surprised all, he swiftly drew his sword and held it above his head. "If there is a land yet unconquered," he boasted, "I cannot rest."

He lowered the sword and lay it flat on the table. "I will be known as the one who defeated the entire world, and kept it in his grasp!"

Kibble took a moment to recover from this outburst. "I'm not a military genius such as yourself, but I do believe you will not be spread too thin if we can keep you supplied with modern weapons." He motioned with his hands. "Your entire border can be secured with just a few men equipped with 21st century weapons."

Alexander signaled his agreement. "The men told me they were tired of moving east. I'm going to announce today that we will be heading back to Macedonia, and then organizing a westward push."

He picked up his sword, slowly running two fingers across the blade. He glanced at Kibble. "You are not entirely correct about the west. We are going to run into some fierce resistance in Germany and who knows what else after that.

But I live for challenge. We are up to the task."

"Just remember," added Kibble, "we are at your service.

Whenever you need more guns or air power, give us the order."

"Oh yes," Alexander was confident, "you will be needed. They will come together and form an alliance against us. You can be sure of that."

That afternoon, Alexander took a helicopter ride with Derek and Kibble. He saw firsthand the destructive power of the aircraft. His confidence was bolstered tenfold, as an entire mountain top fell with one missile strike.

This destructive power was witnessed by his army, which was not far away. His announcement of a western push was well received. They would be homeward bound the next morning.

The time travelers were discussing, that night, what their role would be in Alexander's now unhistorical campaign. Seated in comfortable couches in their living area, they bounced around a few ideas.

"Did either of you realize," Lex piped up, "that we will never be able to live in our own time again?"

"Yes," Derek agreed, "that's true, but it's because our own time destroyed itself. We are on a mission to remake the past and build for a better future."

"Well, at this point," Kibble added, "history can't go anywhere but up."

"So we can keep making trips back to just before the nucs, but we can't stop them?" Lex posed another question.

"Not without significantly changing world events.

That's why we've gone back so far. We really are going to change the course of history."

Derek repositioned himself on the couch. "This is going to blow your minds, but do you realize that the more we alter history, the more different it's outcome will be? Let me put it differently." He explained. "As Alexander conquers Europe, we can keep checking back to our own time."

"That's right!" Kibble was emphatic. "We will eventually find that the nucs will disappear. True, society will never be the same as we are accustomed to, but we'll find something we can live with."

"This is really mind boggling." Lex moaned. "If we go back and find a nuc-free world, but decide to come back here to further develop things...well, the world we return to will be different than the original."

Derek laughed. "The longer we stay and help Alexander, the more different the future will be."

"The question is," Kibble suggested, "how do we know which time period to go back to?"

"Well," Lex concluded, "we can always come back and continue to change events."

Kibble laughed. "We can only do what we can, and hope for the best. For now we are stuck until we can get significant historical changes made."

CHAPTER ELEVEN

The next day the entire army rolled toward Macedonia.

The trip would take two months, so Alexander placed his generals in charge, and elected to travel in the helicopter. The plan was to get back quickly to make preparations for the westward push. By the time his army arrived, he would have raised and trained another small force. The time would also be needed to gather provisions.

Kibble had to stop twice to refuel via time travel. He was concerned about what would happen if he or the others ran into their counterpart selves, going back in time.

However, either by luck or some kind of repulsion, it didn't happen.

Alexander drank in the adventure like a child. The thrill of flying through the sky and visiting other times was so exhilarating, that he had difficulty containing himself. But, like the great warrior and emperor that he was, he took each experience in stride. He was committed to his kingdom, and continuing conquest.

At last the villages and fishing boats of Macedonia came into view. Alexander knew just where to land. Directly in front of the palace they would be the most conspicuous.

He also knew many people here personally.

As the aircraft softly touched ground, not a soul was to be seen. It was evident to him that everyone was hiding. He recalled the way he himself felt when the monster descended from the sky.

Once the engine was off, Alexander stepped to the ground. "Wait here." He called back. "I will return." He walked with a fast and confident pace toward the building.

Thirty minutes passed, and the chopper crew saw no one. They were beginning to get nervous. Derek was in the driver's seat ready to start the engine.

Suddenly Alexander came into view. He was leading a contingent of soldiers and statesmen. As the party approached, Alexander signaled the stop sign. He stepped forward and opened the chopper door. He motioned for the occupants to follow. "Come out." His voice seemed cheerful.

As the time travelers approached the group of dignitaries, their appearance proved predictable. Saucer eyes and gaping jaws were the dominant features.

Alexander introduced them to several important looking men. They all chatted with Kibble, and wanted to look at the flying beast. They all gathered around to look and touch.

Kibble answered each question with sincerity and friendliness.

In the end, everyone accepted them as friends, thanks to Alexander's convincing speech, and, of course, the fact that he was king.

Alexander spoke privately with the flight crew, explaining events as they now stood. Plans remained the same, and he wanted the group to meet the next day to start working out details. Lodging accommodations were made, and the helicopter was guarded for safety.

At the next day's meeting, Alexander was late. He came in with a stressed appearance. After seating himself, he folded his hands, looking at each individual. "This is shocking to me," he began. "I don't understand how the forces from the north could know about my plans to invade. The armies of Germania are approaching, and it appears they are planning an attack."

Kibble was taken back. "How could this be?" He questioned. "History records no force from the north at any time. How could things change that quickly?"

Derek leaned on the table. "Apparently, any changes in history can have dramatic effects. This is most unexpected."

Alexander lifted his arm and pointed to the southeast. "My army is still no less that six weeks away. We'll have to defend this city with 5,000 soldiers. The enemy has about 100,000."

The professor felt his throat tightening. He twisted his mustache in deep thought. Finally he looked up at Alexander and the others. "There's only one thing we can do. We've got one crate of guns with us. Train as many soldiers as we have guns for. We can also use the helicopter's guns and rockets."

He looked at Derek. "You will have to go back for more guns and ammo, while I train soldiers to use them."

Derek made eye contact with Lex. "We'll need to go together." He insisted. "I can't lift those crates by myself."

"OK," Alexander concluded. "Let us go ahead with this plan. But hurry, because we will need the power of the helicopter. The enemy is only two days away."

CHAPTER TWELVE

Lex and Derek walked to the helicopter on a mission to haul weapons quickly. They were escorted by a handful of soldiers, who watched as they boarded and strapped in.

Before flipping on the switch, Derek threw a glance at Lex. "I just have a feeling about this." He wondered aloud. "We may have already changed history so much that we may not find anything familiar to us. Maybe the whole world will be different."

"That wouldn't be good for any situation. "Lex frowned. "Let's hope we can still get weapons and gas."

Derek nodded and pressed his lips together as he flipped the switch.

A few minutes later the whirring stopped and silence commenced. They looked at one another and simultaneously unbuckled their seat belts. The warehouse appeared to still be intact. Derek took a deep breath and stepped out of the chopper. Everything was recognizable! "It's still here!" He tried to contain his excitement.

Lex followed, looking everywhere for signs of changes.

She slowly glided her eyes around, squinting. "Wow." Her monotone voice pierced the silence. She walked over to the kitchen area and peeked in. "Look at this. What's this?" She picked up a strange looking appliance from the counter.

Opening the drawers, she found weird looking eating utensils.

Derek followed, looking hastily around. "I was afraid of this." He muttered, as he jogged back out the door. Running past the helicopter, the stack of crates came into view. He rummaged through one of them, finding weapons, but certainly of a different variety.

He walked briskly back to the kitchen. Lex was just coming out. "What's different out here?" Her voice was strained.

Derek threw his arms in the air. "A lot!" He exclaimed. "The guns are here, but not made the same as the ones we left. The floor and walls are constructed from other kinds of materials. And look, that water faucet is totally odd looking."

Lex went over and counted the crates of weapons. "There are six more crates. That's six trips...and we'd better get started now, before it all gets wiped off the map."

The two quickly lugged one crate to the chopper, and studied the situation. "Let's try and fit two crates in." Lex moved toward the pile. Derek shook his head and followed. They found that it fit fairly easily onto the first crate.

"That's thrifty thinking." Derek praised, jumping into his seat. "Now only two more trips after this." They both strapped in and took off.

The trip back was successful. They unloaded the crates on the ground back in Macedonia, getting help from the guards at the site.

Derek attempted to speak to them in Greek, and was able to say they would be going back two more times. They then repeated the journey.

At the warehouse the second time, Derek decided to check outdoors. The sky was blue, and all appeared to be at peace. He noticed wide variations of cars and houses in the neighborhood that he'd never seen before.

He bravely ventured out to the street and examined a parked car. There were many subtle, but significant differences from the vehicles he was familiar with. Before heading back, he noticed the license plate. It did not signify a state. The lettering was Greek, and said 'The Americas' at the top, with some large Greek numbers.

The trip back was hurried. They had help again with the unloading. Tirelessly, they embarked on a third journey. The final trip was more eye opening than the first two. More household items were 'altered'. Building styles and materials were different. The last two crates of weapons were of a foreign appearance.

As they reached Macedonia for the third and final time, they felt relieved to be able to extract all the weapons, though of different varieties. They did learn some valuable things about how they were changing the future with every action in the year 323 BC.

CHAPTER THIRTEEN

Lex and Derek arrived on time for the meeting with Alexander and Kibble. The Emperor was the first to open the floor. "I am anxious to learn if all the weapons are secured." He looked at Derek.

"We do have them all," Derek answered, "but we encountered some real discoveries. Over the time that it took us to make three trips, the weapons had changed in appearance and style. But everything else also changed."

Kibble perked up. "We have altered the events of time enough to cause such changes?" He was astounded.

"There's more." Derek added. "I ventured outside and saw the parked cars. They appeared like nothing I've ever seen. And the license plates were in Greek."

Kibble twisted his mustache for a moment. Then his eyes lit up. "The very fact that Alexander has remained alive since June 11 has begun to cause significant deviations from the history that we know."

He looked at Alexander. "We can see that even without our help you will be able to conquer Europe, and even America."

"That may be true," Lex interjected, "but if we do help, a lot of lives are going to be saved."

"If you don't," Alexander warned, "we will be destroyed.

We must make plans to defend ourselves. New information says the enemy will reach us in one week."

Kibble nodded. "Yes, you are right, of course. I've trained several groups of soldiers to use guns. Now I can continue by training other groups until the seven crates are gone."

He turned to Derek. "You and Lex will be running the helicopter. Maybe you can avoid massive casualties by simply trying to scare them off. If it doesn't work, you do what you must."

Alexander bore a stern appearance, and spoke directly to Derek. "Warfare is the most serious business of any on earth. If you do not play it to win, you will lose. Do not assume that you are going to scare the enemy into submission. They will surrender only when they have sustained enough losses. I'm telling you, shoot to kill. If you don't, they will kill us."

All Derek could do was to nod in agreement. He looked at Kibble, who was also nodding.

Alexander continued. "We are up against a force of 100,000, with my army 5-6 weeks away. We will have 5,000 soldiers, and the helicopter. We will be depending on the helicopter and 400 men with guns to make the difference."

Kibble shuffled his chair around and spoke up. "We will have about 1,000 grenades as well. I've been training the men to use these too. I think we'll be able to hold them at bay long enough for your army to arrive.

Derek suddenly could hardly contain himself. "I thought we would never be able to visit our own time, in order to resupply ourselves with weapons and gas. But this is what we must do. Go back to sometime before June 11, and from there we can slip back to 2026 and our own time."

Kibble was radiant. "That's the right answer, my boy!

That's why I hired you!"

"If you can keep us supplied, we can hold them off." Alexander sounded reassured. "That will be your job...to fight with the helicopter, then go back for supplies."

Derek agreed. "Lex and I have about a week. We'll get as many supplies as we can."

Kibble twisted his mustache, eyebrows narrowed. "There is a problem there. I will have to go on that mission, since I know where to get the supplies, and it'll have to be me to pick them up."

Alexander chipped in. "I can see we'll need a slight change of plans." His arm thrust a confident blow into the air. "Kibble, you will train me to use all the weapons at your disposal. I, then, will train the men who will use them. That frees up all of you to get as many supplies as possible."

They all looked at one another and nodded in agreement.

"It's early evening now". Kibble peered out the window. "Let's get an early start with Alexander's training. Then we can begin our supply mission sometime around noon tomorrow."

CHAPTER FOURTEEN

Kibble and Alexander went at their training session in earnest the next morning. Loading and firing went pretty easy until they encountered the different variations of weapons from the changing time periods. These took some time, but were fundamentally the same.

At length, Alexander said he felt comfortable, and that the supply mission should commence. They parted company just before noon, and the group gathered at the helicopter.

The professor went over the plan for clarity. Travel to the same spot where they first landed in Babylonia. From there, make the trip back home to 2026, before the world went down the drain. The plan should work...Derek was confident of it.

They strapped in, programmed the computer, and took off. Crash! Whirring stopped. Silence, except for Derek clicking the keyboard for the next stop. "Be sure we really are in Babylonia." He called over his shoulder.

Kibble unbuckled and opened the door. He jumped into a sand dune and walked to the tail of the aircraft. A moment later he was heard climbing back in. "It's exactly as we found it the first time." He remitted. "Guards on the balcony, and everything else."

"Next stop, the warehouse." Derek muttered, as he pushed buttons and keys.

With Kibble buckled in, they took off again. When the noise finally stopped, Kibble opened the door to find the warehouse, just as it used to be.

The lights were on as he stepped down and looked around. The others followed suite.

Kibble walked slowly, heading for the phone in the kitchen. Fifteen feet from the chopper, he suddenly slammed against something. The force of it knocked him back, and Lex caught him in a fall.

Holding his head for a moment, he recovered, looked around again, and scowled. "What on earth was that?"

No one had an answer, so he inched forward, hand out.

Thump! His hands rammed into it again. "Huh?" He exclaimed. "I'm touching something, but it's invisible!"

Derek and Lex came forward and felt for themselves. "Wow," Derek was baffled. "This is solid, whatever it is."

Lex rubbed her hand across the smooth metal surface. She then stepped back, thinking for a moment. Walking back to the helicopter, she felt its smooth surface.

"Guys, I think we're dealing with something that's a lot like this." She continued rubbing the metal surface.

Kibble stepped back, and, as he looked, a faint image came into view. "It is the very same helicopter!" He spread his arms, palms up. "And you can make out a very dim image if you stand back and focus."

Derek was amazed. "So this is our helicopter just before we left the first time."

"Be careful." Kibble warned. "We may run into ourselves, which could be disastrous. We are probably semi- invisible to our earlier counter parts, if this is how they appear to us. Keep your voices down and follow me."

He crept gingerly forward, keeping a sharp eye out for faint moving figures. Reaching the kitchen door jam, he slowly peeked around and viewed the table area. His eye caught a silhouette, which seemed to be one person.

The warehouse door suddenly opened, flooding daylight all the way to the kitchen. It closed, but no figure could be made out. The three of them quickly leaned flat up against the wall. No sounds were made, but there appeared to be motion at the kitchen table. Nothing could be specifically made out, but there was obvious motion at both chairs.

Kibble turned and whispered to his mates, "Lex was at the table, then I came in from outside, then a couple minutes later, Derek joined us. Watch for him."

Not more than a minute later a blur was seen passing through the door. They just waited there at the door jam for about ten minutes. A moving chair would instantly tell them someone was getting up. The silhouettes bobbed up and down, fading in and out. No sound came from the conversation at the table.

Then without warning, all three chairs moved out. That make a loud and clear noise. Up against the wall they flattened once again, watching three silhouettes move out of the kitchen door. The warehouse door then opened and shut.

Kibble stepped away from the wall and sighed. "In case you didn't know, that's what happens when you run into your counter-self in time travel." He stepped into the kitchen and grabbed the phone. "We need weapons and gas ASAP." He made the arrangements and hung up.

"Let's roll, before Alexander blows a cork. He's got to be sweating it out about now." Derek laughed. "No worries. I'll just program our return for when we left!" Kibble slapped his palm to his forehead. "Of course." He smiled.

They slowly pushed the helicopter through the rolled up door, and jumped in. The first stop was for fuel, then onto Kibble's "contact." No one but him knew who the contact was, and he wasn't telling.

They flew for ten minutes before hovering over a large mansion, then landing on a pad. Two men in suites and ties walked out of a garage door carrying a crate. "Leave it running." Kibble called over his shoulder as he jumped out. He handed the men a wad of money, after which they wasted no time hoisting the crate into the cargo hull.

"We'll be back for the other four loads." He shouted to the men. They turned and marched back to the garage door. Kibble slammed the cargo door and pushed on it.

"OK, Derek, take us home to Macedonia." Kibble strapped in while the trip was being programmed.

Momentarily, they were shoved through a time tunnel, and with a loud pop, came out the other side.

Bright sun shown down on them, and the chopper guards were standing in the same spots.

CHAPTER FIFTEEN

It was another tedious five trips from the pickup spot to the warehouse to the capitol building. When the final crate was unloaded, the crew looked up and saw Alexander approaching. Sweat was tricking down his face. He appeared to be out of sorts. "It is very good to see you back." He began. "We must meet...if you would please come with me."

The group bee-lined up to their usual meeting room and sat at the table... except Alexander. He paced the floor a bit before speaking. "First, I am thankful that you have gotten five more crates of weapons." He paced a few seconds more, then stopped. "The enemy is one day away. We must act now to gain the offensive. We cannot allow them to establish anywhere near this city."

He made a fist and held it up against his mouth for a few seconds. "So I have a plan." He continued. "Take the helicopter to their front lines, and shoot the big weapon at them. This will cause panic, and they will run. The men with the guns will be ready to go after them.."

He smiled, looking from one to the other at the table.

He drew his sword and raised it straight to the ceiling. "Then we will go after them with 5,000 men, and they will think we are 200,000. We will route them, and sweep them all the way to the coast."

Kibble cleared his throat to speak, but Lex broke through first. "I'll volunteer to stay on the ground, and let you two pilots go."

Kibble nodded, then spoke. "I really think the plan will work. So we should get started as soon as possible."

"We will begin now." Alexander put on his metal headgear. "But remember, do not return until their entire army is running for their lives."

Kibble stood, nodded his head, and acknowledged the order. "I'm confident we can accomplish this." He and Derek headed for the helicopter, with Lex taking up the rear.

Alexander exited to gather his army and begin the trek to the front lines.

At the helicopter, Lex opened the door for Kibble and Derek, and offered her services. "I've changed my mind about going, if I can be of any service."

Kibble forced a grin. You've always been a great asset, and we do welcome you aboard."

As they were buckling in, he delivered a final briefing. "Hooked to each seat is a backpack with clips and grenades. In the event we go down, we'll definitely need them."

He gave the thumbs up, and Derek started the engine.

The aircraft roared up and over the city of Philippopetis, heading north. Off to the right they could see Alexander's 5,000 men gathering into formation. Derek knew it wasn't going to take long to get there, so he flew slowly, but gained altitude steadily. The terrain gradually inclined to the brow of a hill.

His hands gripped the controls, as he thought about his course of action. He knew the helicopter carried 8 rockets and a set of heavy caliber guns. He couldn't see himself killing thousands of men by firing into their midst as Alexander had suggested. He determined to attempt to scare them off before dealing a fatal blow.

Soon he glided over the summit and caught his first glimpse of the next valley. The sight was eye-popping...a sea of soldiers as far as the distant horizon! Derek didn't hesitate, but acted from impulse. He increased speed as he went into a dive. The front line drew closer and closer. The approach of the army stopped, and seemed to waver back and forth.

The helicopter reached within feet of the line, and zoomed back up. As Derek circled around, he could see mayhem developing.

Again he acted by instinct. He suddenly zoomed to the north, flying low over the army, so as to inflict hysteria from one end to the other. He continued, zigzagging back and forth as he went. The men below seemed to be fighting one another trying to get away.

At last he found the tail end of the force, and did some acrobatics before zooming to the front again. Once at the front, he attempted to herd the entire army back where they came from. He noticed the steep hills on both sides of the valley. Leveling the aircraft, he aimed carefully at the hill to his left, and fired a rocket. It streaked quickly to its destination, causing a massive, earth-shattering explosion.

As if this were not enough, Derek continued flying low, following an irregular pattern. He cut loose with the high caliber machine guns along one foothill, then the other.

The professor and Lex were electrified, hanging on for dear life, yet entranced with the action. Kibble saw the utter free-for-all below, as the chopper raced up and down the valley. He leaned toward Derek. "I think you've got them on the run. Why don't you back off and see what happens?"

Derek nodded, as he circled around and flew back toward Macedonia, gaining altitude quickly.

Upon obtaining a lofty position, he made a small circle, bringing to view the retreating army, traveling at breakneck speed.

Lex patted Derek on the shoulder. "Let's go back. He ought to be happy with these results." Derek turned around and headed back toward the summit.

CHAPTER SIXTEEN

Gliding past the summit, they could see Alexander's army coming into view. Derek brought it down for a landing on a level area in front of the army. Softly touching ground, the helicopter came to rest, and the engine stopped.

The crew welcomed this retrieve, following the furious flight they had just completed. Climbing out of the cockpit, they saw Alexander approaching. He was anxious to hear the story. "Where is the enemy now?" He called out from a distance.

Kibble traveled a few more steps before answering, "You will find them running north as fast as they can go."

Alexander grinned. "We heard a lot of noise, so we knew they must be close."

"I don't know how far away they are by now," Kibble replied, but I know you can catch them. Their numbers are too great to travel very fast."

"You have done well, and I thank you." He stepped to Derek, and placed his hand on his shoulder. "You are skilled with the helicopter. I am indebted to you. But," he faced the three of them. "I will need you to stay close by. We will try to route them with 5,000 men. The front lines will have guns, but we still may need the helicopter."

Kibble nodded. "We'll be there if we are needed...I assure you."

Alexander turned and signaled to his army to go forward, double time. As the army marched on, Kibble, Derek, and Lex looked at one another. The professor finally opened conversation.

"We are going to have to stick with him, I'm afraid. His force is simply too small to get a successful surrender."

Lex showed some misgivings. "So it looks like we'll be staying with Alexander's army indefinitely. If we had a home to return to I would be going back right about now."

"You're not the only one." Derek piped up. "If we went back to our own time now, it would be completely different." "Which is why," Kibble raised a finger, "we'll have to assist Alexander until he conquers Europe. Then we can try going to our own time to see if it's tolerable."

"Well, I can say this much." Lex offered. "I refuse to spend the rest of my life in this primitive existence.

"Don't worry," Kibble assured her. "I, too, am going to leave here as soon as possible."

Derek shook his head. "Do you know it might be years before he conquers Europe?"

"Huh!" Kibble disagreed. "With us helping, it should only be a matter of months."

Lex half chuckled, "I vote to agree with you!"

"And now," Kibble started for the aircraft, "we'd better be monitoring things from the sky."

The threesome took to the air again to assist in rounding up the runaway army.

It took several weeks to finally corner the hostiles from Germania, and a few more thunderous displays from the helicopter.

Alexander finally began the disarming process with his mere 5,000 men. But he set up a station to recruit as many as possible to his own force. This netted him another 10,000 men.

By the time the new men were trained, his regular army of 40,000 had caught up with him. They then began the trek north to Germania to subdue the land and set up taxation, all the while still recruiting.

The helicopter crew was getting pretty good at this new brand of warfare. They set up camp on the outskirts of the main army...associating and having meals with them.

Within two months, they were traveling westward toward modern-day France, which were the Gaulo-Celtic tribes.

At the end of a day's travel, Alexander called a meeting to discuss plans with the helicopter crew. The location was his own quarters, which consisted of a large tent.

The group members were seated in light-weight chairs, in a semi-circle. Alexander lifted clenched fists into the air in a gesture of triumph.

"We have done very well. "He started out. "The lands we have just conquered are what I believe presented the biggest challenge. I do not know the Gaulo-Celtic tribes, but I do know that they are aware we are coming. I think they are afraid, because they know how the Germanic tribes were defeated."

Kibble shifted in his chair. "I have an idea that may save everyone a lot of trouble." He glanced at Alexander, then the others. "As we speak, they are probably scrambling to get an army together. When we approach them, why don't we offer them a chance to surrender."

Alexander quickly drew his sword, and admired it for a moment. Then, slicing twice through mid air, he thrust it back into its sheath.

He nodded at the professor. "I am in agreement, but we must be ready for battle even before we make the offer. You will be close with the helicopter, and the gun division will be on the front line."

Thus, the die was cast for the next chapter of conquest.

The army of 65,000 traveled for another two weeks in a southwesterly direction before any sign of resistance was encountered.

CHAPTER SEVENTEEN

Alexander, who always traveled and fought on the front lines, was the first to get word of a massive army over the next rise. He halted his entire force, and sent for his four generals. He also gave word to get the helicopter up to the front.

Soon Kibble, Derek, and Lex came soaring, and landed on a level spot.

Alexander was just finishing his discussion with the generals at their arrival. "Come!" He motioned exuberantly. "We have a workable plan."

Kibble and company gathered round. "I've sent a man who speaks all languages." He continued. "He is with a small detachment of men, going down the hill right now to propose a peaceful surrender."

He started walking away briskly, then turned around. "Stay close to the helicopter, and be ready." He disappeared into a sea of soldiers.

No more than 30 minutes went by before a commotion arose. The men on the front lines began hollering and thrusting their weapons into the air. Alexander came running out of the crowd. "They have killed our messengers!" He yelled. "The time for talk is over. Go after them, Derek!"

At that, Derek jumped into the cockpit, followed by Kibble and Lex. Within seconds they were floating skyward. The men below were cheering, shaking their spears, swords, and bows.

Kibble and Lex didn't presume to tell Derek what he should do. He had been through several battles, simply reacting to events as they happened.

They jetted over the hilltop, and zoomed into a fearsome scene. Not only were there hundreds of thousands of soldiers, but they were jogging at full speed up the hill, and were nearly on top of Alexander's army! Derek paused in mid flight just for a moment to gather his wits. He then swooped down along the front line of the enemy, nearly low enough to touch the tops of their heads. The line wavered, but continued to race up the hill.

Derek appeared angry as he did a quick loop before firing a rocket directly in front of their line. The explosion was huge, causing them to fall back in utter terror.

At this moment, Derek saw Alexander's men with automatic weapons come racing down the hill firing their guns. Derek then turned and flew low across the center of the enemy. He began zigzagging over the sea of men, nearly hitting them, then swooping into the air. He did a double take, as he saw them drop their weapons and scramble to run away.

He kept up the same tactics, all the way down the line, which he didn't think was going to end. Soon there were groves of trees on both sides. He aimed and fired his machine guns, which mowed off the treetops, which fell onto the soldiers nearby.

After doing the same to the other side, he flew further down the line, where he finally saw the end of the opposing army. Reaching the end, he looped around and fired another rocket into the hillside.

Widespread hysteria resulted, and the men began retreating at a breakneck clip.

During the flight back to the hill, Derek saw none of the retreating soldiers carrying weapons. Their only thought was to run away as fast as possible.

At the hill, Alexander's army was pouring down and giving chase. Derek, Kibble, and Lex all knew the mop-up would take the rest of the day. They flew all around, keeping the edges tucked in, and the fear factor involved.

By the evening, the retreating army had been surrounded and completely disarmed. No more recruiting was needed, so the men were each told to go back home.

The message to each was that taxes would be collected yearly, and that the Macedonian army would protect them.

All the men were shocked and amazed at the flying beast and hand-held guns, against which they stood no chance.

The flight crew met with Alexander that evening, and decided it was time for refueling, and restocking of ammo. The plan for the army was to start out slowly in the morning, heading for modern-day Spain. This area consisted of multiple clans, and may not pose any resistance. Everyone was beginning to feel a sense of relief that the end of conflict was in sight.

CHAPTER EIGHTEEN

The flight crew gathered at the helicopter, this time for a flight through time. Kibble was sure and unsure at the same time. "You know how we have to travel back to the original landing site close to the mansion in order to get back to our own 2026?" Derek and Lex's attention had been attained. "I propose that we do that to get gas and ammo, then see what happens when we take the same zone and coordinates, but travel directly from here."

Lex followed with keen interest. "I would really like to know what our own time is like, considering all the changes we've made in Europe."

Derek agreed. "I wonder what America will be like. I mean, will there be the kind of freedom we are used to?"

"So do you see why we need to check on that now, since we're close to being done here?" The professor summed it up. "We need to know if there is a world for us to live in, since we can't go back to our own world." At that, Kibble stepped into the helicopter, followed by the others.

The trip back to Kibble's warehouse went as usual, followed by the pickup of gas and weapon supplies. They followed the same coordinates every time to avoid running into their counter selves.

Then back to Alexander's army camped at the threshold of modern-day Spain. They unloaded and had soldiers deliver their supplies.

At last they sat in the cockpit ready for the long awaited journey to 2026 to see if they did change the world for the better. Before Derek flipped the switch, the professor delivered a message. "We're going to the location of my house, but we're about guaranteed that it won't be there.

There have been way too many changes."

"Umm..." Derek scratched his cheek. "We can avoid materializing within an object, but isn't it dangerous to not know where we're going?"

"Certainly," Kibble affirmed, "so if we show up in a bad spot, just be ready to send us back." He was silent for a moment. "If anyone doesn't want to take this trip, I will understand. I could go alone."

The flight crew looked at each other. Derek nodded his head. "We're off then." Lex agreed. "It's just something we have to do."

Derek apprehensively programmed the coordinates and flipped the switch. Everyone knew the world would be far from the same, but still was hoping for a tolerable place to live.

Seeming to go on forever, the noise died down finally, and the moment of truth arrived. Derek released himself and stood at the door. Daylight flooded the cockpit, and noise invaded the silence...the sound of engines running.

He looked out and saw several military vehicles...trucks, tanks, etc, at a distance. They were moving directly toward the helicopter. He was alarmed when some soldiers jumped out of a truck and began firing at them.

"Not good!" He yelled, as he shut the door and jumped into the seat. Quickly, he punched in coordinates to return to 323BC, but the computer froze. "Start the motor!" Kibble barked. "We have to get out of here!"

Derek flipped the engine on quickly, and the aircraft began to rise. He throttled it to full speed. Bullets were bouncing off the hull as they sped away.

The surroundings resembled an airport or base as they lifted above it. Moving out as fast as he could, Derek began to see strange sites. People were chained to posts in the middle of the streets. The entire community seemed to be under lock-down, with guards posted everywhere.

They flew higher, which enabled them to see a huge metropolis, and it all looked like detainment camps and prisons.

Kibble leaned forward with a message for Derek. "My guess is that any minute we'll be blown out of the sky. They seem to shoot first, before asking questions."

"So what do you recommend?" Derek questioned.

"We have only one option right now." Kibble yanked on his mustache and scowled. "Take us back to Alexander."

Derek's eyebrows raised. "In flight?" He couldn't believe the suggestion.

"Yes." Kibble reiterated. "I know we haven't tested mid-flight time travel, but I think survival odds are better."

Lex chimed in. "That makes sense, Derek. I'll take that risk to the militant cutthroats around here."

Derek shook his head in disbelief. In that split second, his eye caught a formation of aircraft in the distance. He could see they were quickly closing in. With no further delay, he programmed the return trip. No sooner did he flip the switch, than he saw flashes of light from the approaching aircraft.

The whirring sound began, much to everyone's delight.

Would they complete the trip before being blown to bits? Several seconds of suspense elapsed. The shaking and whirring grew more intense. Then a loud bang sounded, as if they'd been hit. They expected the worst, but instead, the whirring decreased. Everyone looked out the window with uncertainty. Below they saw rolling hills and sparse vegetation.

"We made it!" Derek shouted. The others hooped and hollered in celebration. "We're headed down." Derek announced, as he guided the controls. Soon Alexander's army was in sight, and they glided softly toward the ground. Within seconds, landing bumps were felt, but heart rates still soared.

CHAPTER NINETEEN

The flight crew met and determined to not talk to Alexander about the future, at least for now.

The last section of Europe did not offer overwhelming resistance, but took around two months to subdue because of all the small tribes that did not join together. The helicopter was still busy instilling the fear of God into anyone in its path. Derek served as the chief pilot and Alexander showed much appreciation for his assistance. At one meeting he offered his three assistants high positions in his government if they would continue to complement his great army. Professor Kibble would not turn this offer down. He wanted to continue to influence history in a positive way. His aspirations were to lay the ground work for a free America...the kind he was forced to leave.

Spain was finally conquered, and Alexander had a full plate thinking about his entire empire.

The flight crew tested the future once more, using the mid-flight technique. What they found was worse than before. So much violence and oppression existed that it turned their stomachs. So Alexander's unification of Europe was apparently not the answer.

The professor then called a meeting to come up with the next course of action. Derek drug out three wooden ammo boxes and placed them on the shady side of the chopper. The day was sweltering, and each one carried skins filled with water.

Derek and Lex seemed a bit down after the recent future disaster seen in America. The professor sat and faced them, his hands folded. "So our goal for a strong Europe has been reached," he began, "but our other goal for a free, fair, and strong America has not." He exhaled forcefully, and slapped his knee. "It just occurred to me that we are going about this the wrong way. Don't get me wrong. I believe that Alexander's rule of Europe and parts of Asia will be a good thing. But it's not doing anything for our homeland."

Lex perked up. "Yeah, it seems to me something ought to be done about that."

"That's what I think too." Derek agreed. "Unifying Europe seemed to have a negative effect on America."

Kibble nodded. "We really can't depend on things here to affect the future over there, because we're not going to totally abandon Alexander." He shifted his weight on the wooden crate. "Here's my idea. We need to personally go to the American coast and build from the ground up...make the changes we desire to install."

Lex was stunned. "How do we know what kind of changes we really want?"

"Look at where we are now." Kibble explained. "Alexander's been running roughshod over everybody, and it is reflected in the future...even in America. But we can stop that reflection by our own presence there. That is, by the kind of colonies we develop, and by our relations with the natives."

Derek scratched his face. "Are you saying that we should befriend the Indians instead of conquering them?"

Kibble nodded. "As much as possible. Not all of them are going to allow us to be their friends, but let's push the envelope as far as we can."

"So are you suggesting we begin in 323BC, or move up in time?" Lex questioned.

"Let's give it 2300 years to develop." Kibble smiled. "We may be pleasantly surprised."

"We're still going to need Alexander, though." Derek observed. "We'll need about a hundred men to help us build a fort."

"Good suggestion." Kibble agreed. "And they should be the ones trained to use the automatic weapons. We won't be guaranteed to meet friendly natives. But we will work hard to have friendly relations. Imagine a 21st century America with no Indian reservations, and no discrimination. We can build the country the right way."

During the next meeting with Alexander, Kibble talked about the decision they had made. "Our world of the future lies in ruins, as you know. We must alter the course of events that caused that destruction."

Alexander sat across the table, nodding in agreement. "I certainly understand, but will you still schedule meetings with me?"

"Oh, yes," Kibble assured him, "we will not desert you."

Alexander continued. "My goal is like yours: to bring peace and prosperity to the world. It will be some time before I think of warfare again, except in defense of my kingdom."

Kibble responded. "We will do whatever is necessary to keep your empire secure. This is of great historical importance. But we will be traveling soon to another continent to try to build our country into a strong and peaceful nation."

Alexander placed his hands on the table, looking directly at Kibble, then Derek and Lex. "I have another request to make." He paused for a moment, then held his head high. "I would like to go with you."

Kibble appeared befuddled. He lifted his palms. "You are most welcome anywhere we go, but what of your expansive empire?"

Alexander chuckled. "From here on is building, training, and reinforcing. My generals know that business." He leaned forward, cracking a smile. "And I'm not worried about being taken out of power, having you as a friend. I can return periodically to check on things. No one would dare oppose your weapons."

Derek jumped in. "It would be very dangerous to attempt to build a colony with four people. We really need several families...maybe 50 to 100 people."

"Perhaps you could ask for volunteers among your men." Kibble added. "They must realize that it will be a permanent situation."

Alexander agreed. That will be an easy matter. I know we can find enough families excited to go...but not among my army. Their families are not with the army. Leave this to me. I will get it done."

Kibble nodded, smiling his approval. "Very well, then.

How many days will you need to prepare?"

"One day." Alexander sounded confident. "Let's meet here tomorrow at noon, and I will have your volunteers ready."

CHAPTER TWENTY

The following day, Kibble, Derek, and Lex were amazed.

Arriving at the helicopter just before noon, they were surprised to see about 25 families gathered. At the forefront stood Alexander.

Kibble approached him, gazing in unbelief. "You certainly have an extraordinary talent for organization." He smiled. "May we speak for just a moment to everyone?"

Alexander nodded before turning to wave the crowd forward. The people moved up calmly and orderly.

Kibble raised his arms, palms out, smiling in appreciation. Then, in Spanish, he began to speak. "I truly thank you all for taking a chance at a new life. You are about to leave everything you are familiar with to help us form a new community in a new land. We can travel only four at a time, but it still won't take very long for all of us to get there. Just remember to follow Alexander's orders. There may be hostile natives, so we will be training the men with new weapons. Now we shall begin."

Alexander nudged Kibble's shoulder. He pointed to stacks of crates next to the helicopter. "With each transport we will haul as much food as possible."

"That will be a big help." Kibble returned. "We'll stack them on top of the weapons and ammo boxes." He turned to Derek. "The coordinates are on the computer screen. Our destination will be in Tampa Bay, Florida, near modern-day Safety Harbor. By the way, the year will be 600AD. We don't need 2500 years to get it right."

Derek smiled. "OK, all aboard!" He shouted.

The flight crew took their places with the addition of Alexander. Before stepping into the cockpit, he turned and spoke to the crowd. "It should be only a few minutes, so have the next three ready to go."

He secured himself, then received a gift from Lex...an automatic weapon. "There may be hostile natives." She smiled.

Derek finished programming the coordinates and flipped the switch.

Outside the crowd of volunteers looked on as the helicopter made a whirlwind sound, started to shake, then suddenly disappeared.

In the cockpit the noise died down to total silence. The occupants looked at one another...then as if on cue, grabbed their weapons while in the act of unbuckling. Derek stood and placed one hand on the latch, slowly cracking the door.

Birds chirped, as a warm breeze fluffed up Derek's hair.

He stepped softly to the ground, and walked a few paces. The others followed him.

A strong hint of the Atlantic filled the air. The chopper was situated in a grove of trees, with no sign of life except birds.

The professor moved forward, studying every direction. He shortly came to a clearing and looked around. "We're on a bluff." He announced. "It's a good position." He moved forward a few more paces, when he came to the edge. There it was...the ocean. Something about the beauty or the scent spell bounded them all. Everything seemed perfect.

"Wow," Kibble took a deep breath, "this is a virgin land."

Alexander broke the spell. "If this is the spot, you had better get started transporting the others."

After everyone unloaded the supplies, Derek turned to leave with a parting question. "Do you all have extra ammo?" The team assured him they did, and He hustled into the driver's seat, commencing the transport operation.

While Derek was gone, Alexander led a short scouting trip. He found water right away in the form of a clear stream several feet wide. As they crossed the stream, Alexander held his arms out as a warning. "These droppings belong to a predator, and I've never seen them as large as these."

He backtracked across the stream with the others close behind. As they returned to the landing site, Kibble quizzed him. "So do you think it is bear, lion, or what?"

Alexander bore a puzzled expression. "Really neither one." He shook his head. "It is something new to me."

Before they even arrived at the site, a loud pop pierced the air, followed by whirring that tailed off. The door opened, and three impressed looking people filed out.

Kibble and Alexander unloaded the supplies, and signaled thumbs up to Derek. He wasted no time in setting the Doormac in motion.

It took ten minutes per trip, which would end up taking five hours for 100 people, traveling 3 at a time.

Alexander had some of the passengers help with each unloading. As more people gathered together, he discussed with them their new life. As the weapon pile grew, he did some training of the men to make them competent enough to carry them right away. It was apparent to him that danger abounded in this new land.

Indeed, the mission did take five hours to complete.

Derek finally brought in the last 3 passengers about 5:30pm western European time, which was many hours earlier in Florida.

As the last 3 unloaded, he sat and stared at the computer screen, pressing random keyboard buttons and shaking his head. Shortly thereafter, Kibble popped his head into the cockpit. "Anything wrong?" He questioned, noting Derek's puzzled expression. "Yeah, those coordinates you entered were not for 600AD. Try 60,000BC."

Kibble's jaw dropped. His hands flew up and collided with his forehead. Quickly, he stepped up into the chopper. "Are you sure?" His disbelief showed.

Derek showed him the coordinates and their destination. The location rang true, but the time was off over 60,000 years.

Kibble sat down and stared straight ahead at nothing. "I didn't think we could go back this far." His head continued to shake.

Derek looked at the professor. "Well, the obvious question is what do we do now?"

Kibble leaned forward, resting his elbows on his knees. "I don't know, but this does explain a lot. We have seen droppings from huge animals...not sure what kind."

"We're not equipped to fight dinosaurs." Derek warned. "But at the same time, we can't move these people again today."

Kibble agreed. "During the time you were transporting, we didn't see any animals. Let's talk with the others and come to some agreement."

CHAPTER TWENTY-ONE

Everyone busied themselves setting up camp in the area. Alexander activated a chain of command among the people, and had been busy helping them all. Now he, Lex, Derek, and Kibble had gathered around the chopper to develop a plan of action.

"We have a big decision to make," Kibble opened, "and let me explain it to you."

He twisted his mustache for a moment, and continued. "I had Derek program some erroneous coordinates that sent us to the right place at the wrong time."

Lex and Alexander were both taken back. Hands on hips, Alexander wondered aloud. "Then what year is this?"

"Uh..." Kibble stammered out an answer. "60,000 BC."

Alexander became a statue, whose expression was shock, and speech failed him.

Lex finally spoke up. "How do you know for sure?" "It's a computer entry error." Derek volunteered. "We have to go by the computer. It's been right so far."

Alexander was starting to recover. "Your objective was to make the future better. Where are the people of this age? Can we make a difference this far back in time?"

After a pause and a deep breath, Kibble elaborated. "I would not rule out making a difference in this time period. I think since we're here now, and it took a lot of effort, we should explore the world. We won't know if we can make a positive change until we try."

Alexander raised one hand before he spoke. "The group has been trained well enough with guns to protect themselves. I suggest we do some scouting with the helicopter."

Within 30 minutes they were set to take off. Weapons and ammo were in hand, seat belts fastened. Derek sat at the controls, and with the flip of a switch, started the engine. The volunteer group stood around watching, also with weapons in hand.

Off the ground they slowly rose, then headed inland to explore the terrain. Thick jungle was all around, with clear patches here and there.

It didn't take long to see the animal life, but most was unrecognizable. There were huge beasts that looked more like mammoths than elephants. Great crocodiles were spotted that resembled dinosaurs. They passed numerous large reptilian birds.

After some rolling hills, a big valley appeared with a winding river in the center. Suddenly Lex pointed to the side of the river. "Look, there are people!"

Everyone craned their necks to see several tall, dark toned people dressed in animal skins. As they saw the helicopter, they fled into the jungle and disappeared.

Kibble nudged Derek. "Take it down. We've got to check this out."

Derek floated down gradually, finally landing next to the river. They waited there for a minute, but no one showed. Kibble nodded to shut it down. "Derek, stay here and be ready to start up. The rest of us will get out."

Slowly the three of them unbuckled and stepped out to the ground, gripping their weapons. They moved to the front of the chopper and halted, standing side by side. After another moment of intense silence, Kibble called out. "Hello! We are here as friends."

Leaves rustled at the edge of the jungle. One face appeared, and a man stood up straight, followed by another. They both stood still, tall and lean, dressed in skimpy animal hides. Their braided hair was long and black. Feet were bare, and each man gripped what appeared to be a wooden spear.

No one moved for 30 seconds. The tension was thick.

Finally, Alexander bowed slightly, showing respect. This seemed to have a positive effect on one of the two men. He held a palm up toward the river's edge. He spoke indiscernible words, but was apparently offering seats at the table next to the river.

He began to walk slowly toward the table, his friend following. Alexander and Kibble slowly stepped toward the table, lowering their weapons in good faith. Lex followed.

The two men sat down, and their counterparts followed suit. There were plenty of seats available at the wooden table, the seats being carved out logs.

The visitors gently lay their weapons across their laps, not knowing whether to trust anyone at this point.

The lead native began talking and moving his hands, as though he were using sign language. He seemed to be explaining something.

Alexander's arm jerked just a little. He leaned forward at the waist, an intent look on his face. When the other man finished, he lifted his arms and started returning signs.

Kibble and Lex stared in amazement. The two men across the table smiled and nodded their heads, as Alexander sent out one sign after another. They were grasping at least part of what he was saying.

Then the lead native spoke again while using more hand signals. Back and forth they went...Alexander and the native, for the next 30 minutes, until both were satisfied with the dialogue. Alexander stood, bowing, then gesturing for Lex and Kibble to follow his lead.

The two natives then stood, smiling and giving identical hand symbols simultaneously. Alexander gave the same sign, then turned and strode toward the helicopter. Kibble and Lex quickly followed.

Derek remained at the controls, still on alert. The others filed in to their seats. Alexander hurried them along. "I'll explain later." He said. "Now we must go."

Derek started the engine and began liftoff. The two men on the ground backed off, but stared intently.

Alexander did not speak during the noisy flight, but did make arrangements for a meeting to take place 30 minutes after landing.

Things at the camp had been uneventful. During a brief meeting with camp leaders, he mentioned they would be moving out in the morning.

At the appointed time, the foursome met at the helicopter, and seated themselves in a nearby grassy area.

Alexander opened conversation by explaining his dialogue with the native across the table. "When I was young, my father made sure I had a thorough education. Not only did I learn many languages, but I also was taught what they called 'ancient sign language.' Well, I had no idea it was as ancient as this. I started picking up some of his words, but the sign language was easier to grasp."

"Did you discover anything about them...their needs or wants?" Kibble pressed.

Alexander nodded. "Plenty." He looked around the small circle, and continued. They think we are gods, and are a fulfillment of some kind of prophecy." He let that sink in and went on. They are currently losing a military conflict with neighboring tribes. It's a war that has gone on for hundreds of years. But this is the interesting part." Alexander leaned forward. "They consider themselves pure, noble, and righteous. Their enemy is evil and ruthless, and is about to destroy them."

"I'm starting to get the point." Kibble jumped in. "If we can change this war so that good overcomes evil, the future will be that much better."

"There is another thing to consider." Alexander added. "This group of people we brought with us is going to have to live here. We can't keep moving them around hoping to find a good place. We have to make it a good place."

Kibble agreed. "So if we helped them win this war, their society would eventually incorporate their conquered enemy. The group that came with us would become strong allies of theirs.

Lex added a thought. "I suppose we don't know for sure what will become of the four of us."

"For me," said Alexander, "I will just find out what happens. I am kind of enjoying not being a king."

Derek injected his thoughts. "We all seem to be doing what we feel is the right thing. I suppose when the time comes, we'll see what will happen to us."

"Well, I think this is the right thing to do." Kibble summarized. "Did you make arrangements to meet with their tribe tomorrow?" He glanced at Alexander.

"I did." Alexander was emphatic. "I said we would be back tomorrow, which means most of us will have a long walk. We will set up our own camp outside of theirs."

Kibble nodded. "OK, so let's plan on traveling in the morning."

CHAPTER TWENTY-TWO

The camp was awakened at sunrise by the sound of shots being fired. The flight crew jumped up immediately, running to the source of the noise. Alexander was already there inquiring of his posted guard what the disruption was.

The guard was hyperventilating, and had to sit down, being overcome with fear. Momentarily, he regained his composure, and stood up. "It was a monster of a beast!" he wailed, terror clearly reflected in his voice. "It was coming right toward me, so I shot it, and it ran away."

Alexander gripped his shoulder. "You did well." He reassured him. "Go get some rest before we leave, and send out the next guard."

Alexander turned his attention to Kibble. "We will have to post all 25 guns on the perimeter when we travel. These animals might travel in packs."

Kibble gazed into the woods. "We'll keep watch from the sky, and go after them if necessary."

At length the group was ready to go, and headed west toward the natives' camp. Women and children traveled in the center, while the armed men formed the perimeter. The helicopter would have to travel back to the old camp several times to carry supplies...All the while keeping an eye out for wild beasts.

Derek flew over the river to the natives' camp to get his bearings. He then scouted an area to set up a new camp...an area with a clearing to land the chopper. Adjacent to the clearing was a small lake. The third trip had been completed, and supplies were stacked by the lake. One more trip would do it.

The chopper headed toward the original camp. Derek, Lex, and Kibble were still carefully watching for any signs of danger. The land group was most of the way to its destination, as the chopper flew overhead.

Landing at the old camp, they loaded the last of the ammo and food supplies. They were just stepping into the cockpit when a loud roaring pierced the air. Not more than 30 yards away was a huge aggressive looking animal, focusing his full attention on them. They all jumped into their seats, and Derek started the engine.

The animal then charged straight for the front of the helicopter. Derek knew he would have no time for liftoff.

With the beast moving head-on at them, he engaged the aircraft cannon. Within two seconds the beast fell flat on the ground.

Derek wasted no time in lifting off.

"I've never seen anything like that." Lex exclaimed as they flew by.

The beast's head resembled a lion, its body was that of a rhino, and its tail that of a lizard. Its standing height was about six feet, its length 15 feet.

Derek headed for the land travelers to be sure they were out of danger. Indeed, as he approached them, Kibble spotted trouble. "They do travel in packs! Look to the right!"

Derek saw that three of the beasts were bee-lining toward the hikers, an estimated 200 yards away. He dove to the left and swung to the right, coming in level and straight at the charging monsters. As he closed in, he gave them both barrels. All three were instantly leveled.

As he turned back and flew over the hikers, he could see that they were cheering and waving their arms. He flew in every direction, looking for more approaching danger.

There were visible trails through the jungle, but no signs of life. Finally satisfied, he flew off again to escort the group in to the new camp.

The going was rough through the jungle. Fortunately, some of the men had swords to hack away trails for the rest of the group.

Derek led the hikers into the clearing, and they finally reached their destination. All 100 of them filtered through the narrow trail, dropped their loads at the lake shore, and enjoyed the scene.

The helicopter landed one last time. The flight crew unloaded and sat down for a well deserved break.

CHAPTER TWENTY-THREE

Alexander showed up all smiles, pointing a finger at Derek. "I congratulate you for your flying skill again. I don't know if we could have handled all three of those animals at once. I've seen many fierce predators, but these are a hundred times more so than any of them."

Derek stood up and shook Alexander's outstretched hand. "If I had to live in this place very long," he returned with a grin, "I would go on an extermination campaign."

"Here-here." Lex agreed, as she and the professor both stood to greet the Emperor.

Alexander straightened, hands on hips, facing the helicopter. "We should rest a little while, then fly to the river, just as we did yesterday. All four of us should be there...the same group."

Kibble thumbed the shoulder strap supporting his gun. "I agree we should make a good impression, but I still think we should always carry our weapons. You noticed, the two natives carried theirs."

"And all we saw were two of them." Lex added. "There may be others who aren't so friendly."

Derek grimaced slightly as he spoke. "Do you think it will still be necessary for me to stay in the chopper?"

"Let us see how it goes." Alexander rested one hand on his sword, the other on his gun. "If the dialogue is progressing well, you could join us, but always carry your weapon."

During the 'rest' period, Alexander drilled his security crew about safety. Four guards were to be on duty at all times. The rest of the population was to start constructing rain proof huts from jungle vegetation.

Kibble had brought one 50 caliber machine gun, which he set up and in-serviced several people on. There was a question as to whether the wild beasts could be stopped with small arms if there were more than one of them. This weapon would be a real beast killer.

At the appointed time all passengers were loaded. As the helicopter lifted off, they were prepared for a short, five minute trip. Some apprehension was present because of many unknowns. If Alexander had any misgivings, he didn't show them. He was always the picture of supreme confidence.

Up and over the jungle they glided, down toward the river they soared. There was their destination, and what a surprise met them. The entire river bank was crowded with tribesmen. All were dressed in the same garb. All were tall and slender, with long braided hair. The last commonality was a little worrisome...they all carried spears, except for some with bows and arrows.

As Derek started downward, they made way for a landing spot. Derek looked at Kibble and Alexander. "Are you sure you want to do this?" He queried.

Alexander nodded vigorously. "Sure. It's going to be fine."

Derek swallowed hard and came in for a landing. The Indians kept backing off, the closer he got. On touchdown there was plenty of room. Derek apprehensively turned off the motor. The crowd held their ground.

"I'm staying in my seat, at least for a while." Derek gripped the controls with both hands.

Alexander unbuckled and started getting out. He glanced at everyone. "I know from our encounter yesterday, that we are in no danger. They think we are gods. Let us not disappoint them."

Kibble and Lex grabbed their weapons, slinging them over their heads. Alexander opened the door and stepped out. Kibble and Lex followed.

As they stood by the helicopter, the tribesmen backed up even further. No one said a word, but spontaneously, they cleared a path to the table.

Alexander stepped forward, steadily approaching the table. He noticed the same two men waiting there, who had talked with him yesterday.

When the three arrived, one of the two barked an order to the crowd, waving an arm at them. Immediately, they backed up several feet, and all sat down on the grass.

The man who appeared to be chief motioned for the visitors to sit. Alexander looked to the helicopter, then gave the signal for Derek to come join them. Derek felt more at ease with all the warriors seated, and the orderly progression of events.

While he slowly made his way over, the chief broke the silence. He began an oration accompanied by hand signing. Alexander watched and listened intently, picking up some words, but mostly catching the drift of the sign language. He was so preoccupied, that he didn't notice Derek taking a seat next to him.

The chief's message came out clear, paraphrased thus: "We watched you kill three Puta today. No one ever kill Puta before. No one ever see his carcase before. You must be the gods of the prophecy. You must be sent to save us, the Keota people, from our enemy, the evil ones of the Skeot tribe."

Alexander turned his head to see if the message was dawning on Kibble and the others. It didn't seem to be.

He quickly delivered an answer to the chief, raising his arms to sign. He sent a message confirming the chief's oration...that, indeed, "we are the gods of the prophecy, and are sent to save you."

The chief's eyes grew wide with excitement. He quickly turned and said something to his assistant. The two dialogued for just a short time.

The chief then turned back to Alexander. He emphatically spoke and signed simultaneously. "Our enemy, the Skeot, is very near, and he is preparing to destroy us. If you help us now, we will survive. We stand for everything that is good. The Skeot is everything that is evil."

Kibble was now beginning to pick up on the signing, and some of the language. When Alexander glanced at him, he nodded, giving the OK to offer help.

Alexander faced the chief and briskly signed the return message. "We will find your enemy today. We will make sure that he never bothers you again." He pondered for a moment, then delivered a question. "Where is the Skeot tribe now?"

The chief remained animated. He responded. "They are across the river where the water falls!" Suddenly, he stood up and pointed the opposite direction he had been facing...to the west. He then continued. "He prepares for battle now. He will attack today, maybe tomorrow."

CHAPTER TWENTY-FOUR

Alexander stood to leave, tarrying long enough to sign to the chief. "We go now to fight the Skeots. We will return later." He strode briskly to the helicopter, followed by his cohorts.

Alexander would show no sign of weakness, and made sure his followers didn't either. "Buckle in quickly." He said as he floated into his seat. "Let us find them and scare them so bad they will never come back."

Derek understood that line of thinking, and knew what to do. He started the engine, and lifted off.

Kibble recited what he thought the chief had said. "Across the river where the water falls."

Alexander was impressed. "You have good language skills."

Derek honed in on the mission. He buzzed low across the river, which was wide...about 200 yards across. The other side rose steeply to a bluff about 300 feet above the river. No waterfall was in sight, so he continued gliding up river, just above the surface of the water. They came to a bend in the river, which opened up new scenery.

"Bingo!" Derek shouted, and pointed up to a high water fall. While everyone else was looking up, Kibble peered straight ahead. "Watch out!" He warned. "We have canoes in the water!"

Derek saw them dead ahead. Hundreds of them...large canoes, carrying several men each. "None of them have crossed yet!" Kibble shouted. "Stop them before they get there!"

The chopper was within a hundred yards. Already their shocked faces were apparent. The lead canoes had reached the center of the river. Derek flew low and straight toward them. As he drew closer, the men abandoned ship. It had a domino effect on the canoes in the river. They swam toward shore.

Derek swung around for another dive. As he flew across the river, the entire army was scampering up the trail as fast as they could go. They kept looking up, wide-eyed and scared. They were spinning out across the rocks, dropping their spears and panicking.

The chopper zoomed just over their heads, causing most of them to fall prostrate onto the ground.

The trail led to the top of the bluff, so Derek headed upward. As he broke to the top, the bulk of the Skeot army stood, mouths gaping open. To make an impression, Derek fired a rocket into a vacant hill next to the army. The huge blast sent them all barreling home at top speed. Derek harassed them for a while, shooting at trees and nearby rocks for further scare effects. He then went to a higher altitude, looking for their headquarters.

It wasn't hard to find. A well used trail wound its way through the jungle. Less than half a mile from the bluff, the Skeot dwelling was plainly seen from the air. Its diameter was about ¼ mile. Thatched huts were scattered everywhere. All around the perimeter were sharpened poles, constructed to keep the Puta out.

Derek flew low across the town just to make his presence known. Mostly women and children were present. He turned around to go back and monitor the Skeot retreat. Flying high, he could see the tail end of the army. He then dived to scare them into moving even faster. They were on the move, and nothing was going to turn them back.

"That will keep them away for a long time." Alexander sounded enthusiastic. "Let us go meet with the chief briefly."

Derek smiled as he set a course back to the Keotas. In a few minutes the chopper landed in Keota territory by the river. The chief, once again, was there to welcome them.

At the table, he and his assistant were smiling, as if they had witnessed the great retreat. The chief began signing and speaking immediately. "My soldier see big bird scare away Skeots. We all very happy. You save Keota people."

Alexander signed back, telling about the 100 people he brought with him, and asked permission to set up residence by the lake.

The chief replied in turn that he would like them to stay, and that the Keotas were still going to need protection from the Skeots.

Alexander glanced at Kibble and saw that he was following along. The professor nodded affirmatively.

Alexander responded at once to the chief. "We will stay here to protect the Keotas, and to make sure they remain safe from the enemy."

The chief then stood and turned around, taking something from a man standing behind him. He faced Alexander and place a cord over his head. On the cord were three obviously gold rings. He then signed. "This is 'Presces'... the gift for him who saved the Keotas."

Alexander stood, giving a signal of thanks. He then offered parting words. "If the Skeots return, tell us at once."

The chief promised he would do so, and called to some of his men to bring a final gift. Four men came, each carrying a big basket full of fruit and other foods, setting them down next to the helicopter.

The flight crew made quick work of loading the baskets and strapping themselves in. They took to the air with a feeling of accomplishment and a job well done.

CHAPTER TWENTY-FIVE

The next morning, they began work on their dwelling, opting for one big hut instead of four small ones. The group of families had a head start on them, and offered some pointers about materials and construction.

Alexander's sword was razor sharp, easily hacking down vines and small trees.

As the families finished their homes, Alexander gave instructions on building a perimeter of sharpened poles, as seen in the Keota and Skeot camps. Within two days, all the huts and the perimeter were built.

Everyone was relaxing and recuperating from the stress of the last several days.

Kibble notified the flight crew of a meeting as soon as all could gather in their new hut. An upside down wooden crate served as a table in the center of the room. No chairs were in yet, so everyone sat on the grass floor, leaning against the wall frame.

Kibble opened the meeting. "We need to go back for refueling and helicopter maintenance. We'll also pick up more ammo supplies. But after those things are done, I would like to go back to the altered future to see if the combination of Alexander's campaign in Europe, and our little scuffle here did anything."

He paused for a minute, then continued. "All who want to go along raise your hand." Everyone raised their hand.

"OK," Kibble chuckled. "Maybe this is a good time to make a point clear. If we happen to find a world that anyone is comfortable in, they are welcome to stay there."

"I guess I'm searching for a place and time far less primitive than this." Lex confessed. "I mean, I was having a hard time in 323 B.C.. Here we are in 60,000 B.C.."

Derek raised one hand. "I've come to the conclusion that we'll never get back to the world we knew, no matter what we do. We should try to find one that's civilized and modern. Am I assuming everyone wants modern?

Alexander chuckled. "I really do not have much of an idea about your modern world, but I am anxious to find out. I always desired only to be the Emperor of the world. I am now finding that I do not want to go back to that. The only time I was actually happy was getting drunk at the end of a campaign. I think it is a good idea to find a modern and civilized world that will make us the happiest."

Kibble seemed pleased, as he changed position and took a deep breath. "I guess that is what I wanted to find out...where you all really wanted to end up."

He stroked his mustache with one hand, briefly pausing. "Well then, we'll plan to visit the altered 2026 in two hours.

That's how long it will take Derek and me to service and refuel.

True to his word, Kibble and Derek were back with 15 minutes to spare.

As Alexander and Lex gathered round, Kibble spoke up. "The world in 2026 is the same as always. Businesses are booming right up to the nuclear attacks. Now we'll see how the altered 2026 will be. If it's not to our liking, we'll go back to the drawing board."

Everyone buckled in, weapons in hand. "By the way," Kibble mentioned to Derek, "we'll try Chicago, then New York City. In the city it's safer to enter during mid-flight."

"Check." Derek returned. "We're taking off then." The engine fired up, and the aircraft lifted straight up.

The elevation continued until Derek had gained enough altitude to clear the highest sky scraper.

He looked around and signaled thumbs up. "Here we go." The doormac began its whirling motion, and before long, they had exploded onto a different horizon...one with buildings and streets.

"Still doesn't look like Chicago." Derek muttered. "We're going down for a closer look."

As he dropped lower and lower, it became evident that nothing had changed since their last visit. It was basically a mass of prisons. Public chainings were seen all over the streets. There were barbed wire fences and flood lights everywhere.

Quickly Derek began programming the trip to New York. "If my guess is right, they'll be coming after us any minute."

Kibble peered out the window. Sure enough, a distant group of aircraft was approaching...rapidly. "Here they come!" He shouted. "Get us out of here!"

Derek didn't need more prodding. He slammed the switch, starting the doormac in motion. As the whirring grew intense, Kibble saw flashes of light coming from the approaching aircraft. He knew missals were on their way, but the whirring climaxed and exploded, bringing a new horizon into view.

"That's the last time we're going there." Kibble wiped the perspiration from his brow. Derek started lowering altitude. "Don't know if this will be any better, so keep alert."

As they came closer to the ground, things were looking like a normal metropolis. Streets with odd looking vehicles on them, attractive subdivisions.

Derek saw a vacant parking lot and headed for it.

There were no signs of prisons or police. The chopper came down softly in the center of the lot. He left the engine running for a moment. Soon a man dressed in a suit came out of the building, adjacent to the lot, and began walking toward them. Derek shut off the engine.

Kibble started to get out. "Stay here," he said, "and be ready to take us back to camp quickly."

He and Alexander stepped out of the aircraft and approached the man, making no attempt to hide their guns. The man stopped to greet them, offering a hand shake to both. "Hello." He said in English. "How can I help you?"

The two travelers were surprised. "English." Kibble revealed his ignorance. "We weren't expecting that."

"My name is Reverend Jacobs." The man replied.

"English is spoken in this sector." He hesitated for a second. "So what's going on here? I've never seen a flying machine like that."

Kibble held up both hands. "Let me be honest with you.

We are time travelers. The first question I have for you is...are we safe here right now?"

The Reverend was taken back, and at a loss for words. "Uhhh...yes, but I wouldn't tarry long. Where and when are you from?"

"I'm from the United States of America, which takes up this entire continent. My time period is the same as yours, but occupies a different time thread. In other words, we changed history, and you are the result of it."

Reverend Jacob's eyes bugged out. "I've always sensed that something was wrong. Let me ask you: how do I know you're speaking the truth?"

"Watch the helicopter." Kibble declared. "When we leave, it won't fly. It will simply disappear. We are heading back to 60,000 B.C.." He stepped closer and gestured as he spoke. "Please tell us...how much liberty do you have in this district?"

The Reverend stroked his chin in thought. "Well, I can tell you we can't do anything without the government's OK. If you do get caught, you are sent to prison, and may never get out."

Kibble nodded. "Yeah, we've already seen that. Look, we've got to go, and I thank you for your time."

The two men turned to leave, but were called back by the Reverend. "Please wait!" His plea was in earnest. "Please take me with you! I've got to get out of this place. I can do a lot of things, and will be a real asset to you."

He gripped Kibble's arm and implored again. "I promise you won't be sorry."

Kibble seemed at a loss for words. Alexander then broke in, making eye contact with Kibble.

"Let us take this man. He will prove his worth. I am a good judge of character."

Kibble sighed. "You'll have to sit between two chairs.

We'd better get going."

CHAPTER TWENTY-SIX

Reverend Jacob's face lit up as he scampered toward the helicopter with the others. He was ecstatic to introduce himself to Derek and Lex. "Hello, I'm Reverend Jacobs, but call me James." They nervously acknowledged his greeting while everyone buckled in.

"Back to camp." Kibble snapped. "It's not safe here."

Derek already had it programmed, and simply flipped the switch. Lex leaned over to the Reverend. "Hold onto something. We'll be doing a lot of spinning for a while."

James gripped two seats, as they floated off the floor.

The whirring and spinning started out strong, causing him to grit his teeth and hold on for dear life. Then he felt vibrating, and soon a high pitched noise, followed by a boom.

Everything decelerated, winding down to total silence.

James opened his eyes and relaxed his grip. Out the window he could see jungle and sunlight.

Alexander's voice broke the silence. "Meeting at the hut in 30 minutes."

Everyone went in different directions, leaving James standing next to the lake taking in the sights.

"It's probably hard to grasp all this happening so suddenly." The Reverend turned to see Lex, who was trying to be a stabilizing agent.

"Oh..." he replied apprehensively. "Yes, I never thought time travel was possible." Taking a deep breath, he continued. "But when a chance presented itself, I wasn't going to not try for it." He chuckled. "Really, anything would be better than the life I had there. The government meddled in everything, including religion."

Lex shook her head. "That is entirely our fault. Our world was destroying itself with nuclear warfare. We escaped just in time. Our goal was to create a stronger Europe to alter the balance of power. We chose to join Alexander the Great in 323 B.C.. Well, mission accomplished, but your world is the unintended result of the conquering of Europe."

James looked puzzled. "So in your world, Alexander never defeated Europe?"

"No." Lex replied. "In fact, he died in 323BC. We came just in time to prevent him from death following a wine binge. If you are a historian, you may want to speak to him. He sat next to you in the helicopter."

James froze in unbelief. "That was Alexander the Great?"

Lex nodded. "And believe me, he is great. He can figure anything out, or convince anyone of whatever he wants."

"So what are you all doing this far back in history?"

Lex smirked. "It was a mistake. We were trying to go to 600 A.D., but Derek programmed 60,000 B.C. accidentally. We had transported 100 people from Europe, and it was too hard to move them again, so they are staying. Derek just won a battle for a chief whose tribe is right next to us."

James looked at the helicopter. "So that is a military aircraft, I assume."

"Yes, that's what got us this far." Lex replied. "Overwhelming power versus swords and spears."

"And how did you get involved with this time travel mission?" James queried.

Lex laughed under her breath. "It started out when I answered Kibble's ad for a part time job keeping books for his scientific experiments, plus doing housework. When war started, I ended up going along with him and Derek. Derek actually worked for him in the lab."

James nodded. "I'm getting the drift of the situation now. So what's next on the agenda?"

"That" Lex proclaimed, "is what our meeting will be about. We went to the year 2026 twice now. Both times we were attacked by aircraft, as well as tanks and guns. We need to figure out how to change history in a positive way."

The meeting commenced at the appointed time. All five of the participants gathered inside the hut. Reverend Jacobs got more acquainted with them, as he was a good conversationalist.

Kibble officially opened with food for thought. "Our past attempts at improving American history have failed. We need some ideas about approaching this dilemma. That is why we are here."

Alexander picked up the train of thought. "I believe that 60,000 B.C. is too far back to have any effect on modern events. We need to come in just prior to the formation of America as a nation."

Derek chipped in. "Probably about 1500 A.D. would work. It's just before most of the Europeans started arriving."

Lex added. "That sounds good, but I think trying to fight wars is having the opposite effect that we want. We should think of ways to help people and gain their trust."

"And that's where I come in." Reverend Jacobs raised one finger. "My specialty would be to head up a mission.

First to heal and feed the body...second to feed the soul. I can promise a great gathering of people, and great popularity for all of us."

Kibble lifted his head higher and a smile crept over his face. "That's it!" He declared. "We'll change history in a positive way!"

Alexander cut loose with a belly laugh. "This man has the right idea! My life has been dedicated to conquering and imposing my will. If, however, we want historical peace, we must be kind and helpful. We must make them want to be our friends."

Kibble looked at Alexander. "I do see where your skills would be invaluable, however. When the settlers come in and start killing Indians, we'll need a strong military, and a set of laws to keep the peace."

James spoke up. "I can even see you establishing a new kingdom based on fairness to everyone, but with a strict set of laws. Where I came from we had the strict laws, but no fairness."

Alexander drew his sword and jabbed it into the ground, while still sitting cross-legged. "This is going to be a great challenge, and a lot of fun! I will rule the land, but will maintain fairness and equality to all men."

Kibble clapped his hands. "We have enough to get started on. Can we leave in the morning?"

Alexander nodded. "The group that came along with us will have a choice of staying or coming along. That seems fair. I think we also should come back here periodically to check on the Keotas to be sure the Skeots are not planning another attack."

Kibble agreed. "We should fly over their camp once before we leave to get a feel of what's going on there."

CHAPTER TWENTY-SEVEN

The next morning Alexander learned that the group of 100 preferred to come along to the 15th century. This was because of the dangerous animals and fierce natives. They also liked Alexander, and wanted to join with him wherever he went.

The first mission of the day was to fly over the Skeot camp. To their surprise, there was no sign of them, and it appeared they had totally abandoned their camp. This news they brought to the chief, whose spirits were greatly lifted.

Alexander explained that they must move on to urgent business, but they would return within a week to check on the safety of the Keota tribe.

The five returned to camp and began preparations for the move to the 15th century. They would travel there first, then be able to take four people at a time because of a make- shift chair that was fashioned for James.

The Reverend tried to turn down carrying a gun, but reluctantly took an in-service in case he ran into dangerous animals.

The first few groups were gathered, as the starting five sat, ready to transport.

"We are going to 1500 A.D.." Kibble started the briefing. "The modern location will be the eastern part of North Carolina. The is along the coast line. The reason we chose this area is because the Indians are the most civilized and progressive of the known tribes. The Cherokee are close by, and they are the largest of the tribes. Historically, they were friendly until the gold miners trespassed their land. We are arriving before the time of any European voyagers, except Columbus, who they never saw."

Alexander offered a thought. "One thing to keep in mind. You are going by history as you know it. With the changes we made in Europe, I expect their history to be much different. We really don't know what to expect with the Europeans."

"Point taken." Kibble nodded. "So I think we're ready, unless there are any questions."

Derek placed his hand over the switch. After a short pause, he flipped it. As the noise and motion started, everyone's minds were fixed on what may be in store for them around the corner.

The racket finally climaxed and came to an end.

Getting their bearings, they all peered out the window and saw trees.

Derek took the lead by unbuckling, grabbing his weapon, and standing. After eye contact with the group, he opened the door and cautiously stepped down. The others followed suit until all 5 stood in a lush meadow near a grove of trees. They slowly strayed a few steps from the helicopter.

Alexander's ears perked up, as he turned his head to the left. He held up his hand. "I hear voices coming from this way." He pointed.

Everyone gripped their weapons while scrutinizing the horizon. The voices grew stronger. "Get down!" He waived his arm and crouched down.

As they all squatted in the tall meadow grass, the silence was suddenly shattered. An enormous creature barreled around a nearby tree, running directly toward them. It let out a deafening roar, shaking its head back and forth.

Knowing a collision course was inevitable, Alexander stood, opening up with a machine gun blitz. The others came to their senses and joined in. The animal sprinted to within ten feet before collapsing, causing a small earthquake. As the shocked gunmen stood petrified, Alexander forced words from his lips. "I never realized bears got that big."

From around the same tree came a group of ten men, some carrying swords and some bows and arrows. All had the appearance of European settlers.

The men stopped in their tracks when they saw the unusual sight. They seemed frozen for a moment, then one of them, with a thick beard, stepped forward slowly. Seeing the dead bear, he placed his sword in its sheath. He stared at the helicopter, and the five strange visitors. He slowly raised his hands before speaking. "Hello." In English. "We mean no harm."

Alexander advanced gradually toward the stranger, one hand still on his gun. As he drew near, he returned the greeting. Raising one hand, he halted within six feet. "Hello. My name is Alexander."

The bearded man pointed at Alexander's gun. "You killed the bear with weapons I've never seen before."

Alexander held it up and acknowledged. "It is called a gun. It is a weapon of the future. Let me tell you the truth. We are time travelers, and are from different periods of history."

The man didn't flinch at this news. He repositioned he feet, taking a deep breath, then answered. "I'm inclined to believe you, but there are those who would call you a witch."

Alexander laughed heartily, throwing his head back. "I have been called a lot of things, but that is not one of them. Let me just say this. Our intentions are to be your friends. Is there a place we can meet to talk?"

CHAPTER TWENTY-EIGHT

The bearded man nodded. "Yes, we have a settlement just east of here."

Kibble turned to Derek. "Can you start transporting people? We'll be back to tell them where to set up camp."

Derek returned to the Doormac, while the others followed the group of men.

After five minutes they arrived at the settlement...big enough to be called a town. Log cabins lined a street, which extended for as far as they could see.

The four time travelers were a spectacle as they walked through the main street. By the time they reached the town hall, quite a crowd was following along.

Inside were plenty of benches and tables. The bearded man and his associates sat down. The travelers found a bench facing them and sat.

The apparent group leader then introduced himself. "I am Captain Dickie. We came from England one year ago.

The Indians have been friendly, but we've had a lot of trouble with bears. I would like to have weapons like yours."

Alexander smiled. "We can take care of your bear problem. I need to know if we can stay nearby. We have over 100 people."

"Surely there is plenty of room." Captain Dickie spoke enthusiastically. "Can you tell us about yourselves? Where are you from?"

"The others can speak for themselves, but I came from the year 323 B.C.. My name is Alexander. You may know me as Alexander the Great."

"I don't know why I believe you, but somehow I know it's true. I've heard stories about your conquests. But when you took Europe, you used some strange, but very effective weapons...about like the ones you have now."

Alexander smiled, and in a flash, drew his sword. He held it straight up in the air as he stood. "This is still my favorite weapon." He glared at everyone in the room. The sword then found its sheath, and Alexander his seat. "But I couldn't have gotten nearly as far without my friends from the 21st century." His right arm made a sweep toward Kibble and Lex.

Alexander eyed Captain Dickie. "I have a proposition for you." His gaze swept over the entire 16th century group, including the onlookers in the packed hall. He continued. "I'm going to start a peaceful militia. This land is going to turn into a powerful, but peaceful and fair nation. And we are going to start it right here."

There was a buzz throughout the entire hall. It went on for a couple of minutes before Captain Dickie stood, holding up his hands. The noise settled down.

"Alexander the Great, you and your friends are welcome here. Please help us get rid of these pesky bears, and you can do anything you see fit."

Alexander stood once again. "I'm going to post guards around the town to kill or run off the bears. Meanwhile, we are all going to build a wall around this settlement to protect you from man and beast."

He gestured with both hands. "Right now if anyone wants to witness the time machine in action, you are welcome to follow us."

Everyone cheered as they started clearing the hall to gather again on the street. Alexander's powers of motivation were apparent to all. They saw clearly why history's account of him was so great.

The whole town, it seemed, followed along while Alexander led the way back to the helicopter. Captain Dickie pushed his way up to Alexander, and began conversing.

"Would it be possible for me to travel in the time machine just once?" He implored.

"I assume it would," Alexander replied, "but it's not my machine. You must speak with professor Kibble."

Kibble, who was on Alexander's other side, leaned his head forward. "Certainly, Captain. You'll be on the next trip. We're going back and forth to the year 60,000 B.C.."

On arrival to the landing site, there was no helicopter, but a small group of people stood waiting for the aircraft's return.

Alexander ushered the townspeople to withing 30 feet of the reappearance site. He faced the crowd and held up his arms. "This is the location. Momentarily, you will see a flying machine that will appear right in front of you. It will be arriving from a location hundreds of miles to the south, and 75,000 years ago."

The people appeared to have no concept of what he was talking about. Their faces reflected confusion, and most of them were more interested in the bear carcass than waiting for a suddenly visible object.

Filling the entire meadow were about 200 people from the town. All were curious onlookers who knew that something strange had happened, and was about to happen again.

Captain Dickie was on the front line, eagerly glancing at the designated site. A sudden rift and boom jolted the onlookers, who, in an instant, were staring at the helicopter.

Vocal exclamations were forthcoming, as they witnessed something the likes of which they'd never dreamed of before.

Captain Dickie, overcome with excitement, was barely able to stumble forward to ensure himself a spot on the trip back. Kibble followed him, as Alexander diverted to talk to families who were recently transported.

Derek and passengers piled out of the cockpit, opened the cargo door, and began unloading belongings.

The buzz in the crowd continued while Kibble showed Captain Dickey the aircraft and Doormac. Derek accepted Kibble's offer to replace him for a while.

Buckling Captain Dickie into his chair, the professor quickly reviewed the programming and secured himself. He glanced over his right shoulder. "So are we ready, Skipper? I'm going to engage the switch."

Dickie, still trembling and ecstatic, managed to nod his head. "Eye," he took a deep breath, "let's go!"

Dickie became mesmerized by the whirring sound. He grabbed his head to lighten the dizziness. The intensity grew, seeming to last forever, when an explosion occurred, followed by a winding down of the noise and circular motion.

Kibble unbuckled himself, and showed Dickie how to do the same. From outside he heard a commotion, so he grabbed his weapon and cautiously opened the door.

CHAPTER TWENTY-NINE

There to meet Kibble were several men who frantically spoke to him in Spanish. "Quick! The Puta has broken down the barrier, and the big gun has jammed!"

Kibble jumped out and followed the men. Captain Dickie just stepped to the ground, surveying the situation.

The men had the 50 caliber gun set up on the ground, so Kibble rushed over, first checking the ammo belt. He flipped switches and released clips until the jam cleared.

Flopping on the ground, he pointed the barrel at the entrance of the camp barrier. There he could see a puta crouching, and looking as if he were going to pounce any second.

Several men had automatic weapons, but were afraid to trust them, considering the size of the beast. To make matters worse, they could hear at least one more puta behind the first one.

The women and children were cowering against the fence. The men stood in front of them carrying guns.

Creeping forward, the first puta inched his way into the camp. On cue, the men began shooting, which only angered the animal. It ran forward at the men, who continued firing. The gunfire finally halted the creature, which collapsed and rolled over.

This, however, cleared the way for two more puta to belt through the opening. The men had used up their ammo, and were rushing to reload new clips, but the puta were bolting toward them.

Kibble took aim and pulled the trigger. Down went the first beast in front of the desperate men, who couldn't reload in time.

The second puta saw kibble, and changed course toward him. While the men were still reloading, Kibble took careful aim and let him have it. The monster was so fast that it nearly reached him before being blasted to the ground.

The men with guns stood motionless, thinking there would be more puta coming through the narrow opening. Kibble didn't move a muscle for the same reason.

Captain Dickie was leaning against the helicopter, both arms flat against the side.

A moment later, Kibble stood and briskly paced over to the men who had fought for their families' safety. "You will have to stay while your families travel first in order to protect them." They all agreed to do so, even though they were scared half out of their wits.

"Which one of you was trained on the big gun?" One man stepped forward. "I was trained, sir. My name in Gavante."

"Good." Kibble went on. "You can test it with me. The rest of you barricade that hole to keep them out."

The men quickly found branches to pile at the entrance.

Gavante successfully fired the 50 caliber gun, which was Kibble's cue to get going.

After choosing three passengers, he and captain Dickie loaded their luggage and boarded.

Alexander watched as the chopper reappeared. His anxiety level suddenly diminished after the lengthy wait. He was there to greet the passengers and point them in the direction of the other family members. All luggage unloaded, he turned to Kibble and Dickie. Seeing their ashen faces, he knew something had gone wrong. "You are late getting back, and look as though you just saw a ghost."

"We had a puta attack." Kibble offered, as he opened the cockpit door. "I didn't have time to explain anything to Captain Dickie, but no one was hurt. I've got to transport the families as fast as possible."

He jumped in and closed the door.

CHAPTER THIRTY

As the helicopter disappeared into thin air, Captain Dickie and Alexander stood staring at nothing.

"We will need to get started right away." Alexander broke the silence. Dickie nodded as he pursed his lips. "And by that I assume you mean to build your housing and get settled."

"That is true." Alexander started walking in the direction of the settlement. "But I need you to designate the land that is to be used."

"That I can do if you will follow me." Dickie picked up his pace.

As they walked, Alexander explained more about his plans. "My goal is to build a kingdom." He spoke unabashedly. "I will not lie to you. I, myself, will rule the kingdom. I do not say this out of selfish ambition. But it is the truth that I know how to build an army and rule a people. I am determined to form a government that will be fair to all men."

Dickie continued to nod and patiently listen. Alexander went on. "The good thing about this is that it will provide immediate employment to those who join my force. It will not be mandatory, but many will join for sustenance."

Dickie spoke with a new found conviction. "You know I've heard rumors that some Indians are not happy that we are here. We really do need a definite force for security. I for one will support you. I think we should join forces and build your kingdom."

Alexander turned and placed his hand upon Dickie's shoulder. "We should indeed do that." He spoke with inspiration. "We shall organize right away...at the same time building homes, then a walled city."

As the two men approached the town, Dickie pointed. "Across the road is a trail that leads to a forested area.

There's a lot of room there, and a creek runs through it."

Alexander crossed the street and eyed the trail. "This will be fine." He decided without delay. "Have your men meet me at the town hall this afternoon. I will go over plans with them."

The transporting progressed well. Kibble grew tired of the grind, and placed Derek back in the driver's seat.

Most of the passengers had been transported. Kibble, Lex, and Reverend Jacobs were standing around the site, briefing and directing the passengers as they arrived.

Alexander had taken a large group of them over to the construction site to set up camp and begin work. He had explained to everyone his plan to set up a kingdom and build an army.

Reverend Jacobs found himself busy speaking with the transportees, as he knew some Spanish. He and Kibble handled the briefing and luggage, while Lex took care of medical needs, which was one of her skills.

The time came for Derek to transport the last group, which included the 50 caliber machine gun. As the chopper appeared, the trio moved in to help. Derek swung the door open, and the grueling task had finally come to an end.

The passengers looked weary, and so did Derek. When their belongings were unloaded, James began updating them on events, and personally led them toward the building site.

Everyone gravitated to the new site, leaving the chopper unattended, which Derek and Kibble vowed to rectify ASAP.

They soon found the entire group standing around Alexander in a clearing. He welcomed the final handful of members, and went into a recap for their benefit.

"This, we hope, will be our permanent home. Captain Dickie loaned us several wood cutters, and we will begin immediately cutting trees for log housing. I must go to the town hall to meet with their men. We will form another branch of military defense. Yours speaks Spanish, and theirs will speak English."

Alexander then broke up the crowd, saying they should help one another by cutting trees where the housing will be. He asked that Kibble and Lex come along with him. Kibble assigned Derek and James to clear an area for the helicopter and then move it right away.

On the way to the town hall, Alexander posed a question to Kibble. "I am going to need a second in command. Would you be willing to take the job?"

Kibble thought for a moment before answering. "I would be honored, but I have one request. May I have three assistants? They would be Derek, Lex, and Reverend Jacobs."

Alexander cut loose with his patented belly laugh. He drew his sword and cleared away some brush with one sweep. "Of course it is important to have trusted assistants." He looked at Kibble and Lex. "Yes," he agreed, "all three are worthy." He sheathed his sword as he stepped onto the street.

Kibble offered one more question. "How easily will we acquire new recruits to the army?" Alexander stopped and faced Kibble. "I am never concerned about that. They will come from everywhere. Ships from Europe... even Indian tribes that want a better life."

Kibble smiled and continued walking. "I never doubted you, but I was just curious about your plans for growth."

Alexander picked up the pace. "I've never had a problem with that." A confident smile showed under the beard.

CHAPTER THIRTY-ONE

The three reached the town hall, which was packed with standing room only. Captain Dickie was at the door waiting for them. He seemed happy to see them, and ushered them to the front of the room. Kibble and Lex found chairs, but Alexander preferred to stand. He gazed at the packed crowd and paced back and forth briefly. Resting his right hand on his sword, he spoke. "We are here about important business. And that is safety and peace. In order to enjoy peace, you must be ready for war. We must be strong. Make no mistake. We are seeking peace and tranquility."

He paced back and forth a few times, then lifted his head once more. "Not only will you be at peace, but I will offer you food and shelter. Join with me and your families will be safe from man and beast of any kind."

A buzz ripped through the room as everyone was sitting on edge. Finally one man stood to speak. He was a giant of a man...about 6 feet and 10 inches tall. His hair was to his shoulders, and so blond that it reflected light.

He raised one arm and made a sweeping motion across the hall. "Let everyone take note that I am the first to join this man. We should all give him support, and I, Jens, offer it to him now.

One after another, they stood to grant allegiance.

Alexander's bearing commanded respect from all. His presence attracted support and excitement. The crowd pressed from all sides until finally he held up both arms for silence. "Those who would join me shall meet here tomorrow morning. We will get organized and begin our successful journey to greatness!"

A loud cheer erupted, and it took several minutes for the crowd to begin to disperse.

On the way back to camp, Alexander went over some things with Kibble and Lex. "This has gone very well, just as my first military organization did. The only difference is we had more population to draw from in my beginnings."

Kibble took a keen interest. "That may not be a problem. It seems that with the altered history, more ships have come from Europe, even at this early date. According to Captain Dickie, there are settlements all up and down the coast line."

Alexander was clearly excited over the news. "This will really speed up our progress." He exclaimed. "When we get our fort completed, we will go on recruiting trips."

Turning his attention to Lex, he continued. "And Lex, we will need you tomorrow and on all recruiting trips to keep a record of personal information." He hesitated. "Now this sounds like you don't have much importance, but really, you will be one of the top people in our government."

Lex laughed. "No, really the whole thing sounds like a lot of fun. I don't mind doing this at all."

As they approached the campsite, it was clear that the men had been working very hard. Derek and James hurled a crosscut saw, and had cleared a large area for the helicopter. The others were spread out all over the valley clearing for their homes.

Derek stopped and stood when he saw the group approaching. James stepped forward, anxiously awaiting word of the meeting. He sensed a buoyant spirit in them. "So what tidings do you bear from the big event?"

Alexander stopped and admired the clearing and piles of logs all around. "You are making real progress here."

He swept an arm across the horizon. "In the morning we will organize the townspeople into an army. We will delegate some to construct weapons, while the rest will build houses."

James smiled as he slapped his hat across his knee. "It sounds like a success story, then. I intend to have a church built, with a medical station in or around it."

Kibble nodded vigorously. "I like your plan. That's exactly what this community needs."

Derek stepped forward. "Right now I'm headed over to move the helicopter into this spot."

The professor smiled. "Couldn't agree more." he answered, dealing a quick pat on the back as Derek scooted by.

Alexander continued where he left off. "The way it will work is like this. Everyone will have a particular job to do.

I'm talking about all of you who are going to be leaders. Kibble, as second in command, you will delegate and work with the other leaders. James, you will run the religious and medical sides of things. Lex, you will do organizing, and assist with medical. Derek is brilliant with science and machinery. He can continue this. Captain Dickie and Jens would both make good military leaders. We need to find someone who is good at handling food and cooking for an army. As we have other needs, we will assign someone to deal with them."

CHAPTER THIRY-TWO

The following morning all the leaders arrived at the town hall to find that the building was mostly full. As they walked in, everyone was quiet, but eager to begin.

Alexander stood in the front, facing the audience. "Welcome all of you, and congratulations for joining the first army of a country that will become the greatest on earth.

Our members are going to grow very rapidly, and you will discover the many benefits of being the first to join a fine fighting force."

He paused while pacing ten feet to the right. With a quick left face, he addressed the crowd again. "I would like to introduce the members of the cabinet...the government leaders."

He started with Kibble, saying a few words about him, and continued to Lex, James, and Derek.

At this point, he again faced the people squarely and spoke. "I would like my two generals to come forward. Their names are Jens Brock and Richard Dickie."

The two men had prior knowledge of this, and were prepared to be called up front. They both rose and stepped forward together. Alexander stood next to them, while the cabinet members took their seats.

"These two men will lead different branches of the army. However, as you know, I have 35 men who speak only Spanish. I will take personal responsibility for them. The other branch is right here, and you number about 74 men.

You will be under the command of General Dickie. General Brock will get his own command, but until then, he will assist General Dickie."

I understand that General Brock is an expert archer, and can also make the bow and arrow." Glancing at General Brock, he continued. "You will need to begin constructing as soon as possible, and train a group of men to do the same."

He scanned the entire assembly. "When our homes and fort are finished, we will travel along the coast to other settlements. We will recruit as many as we can." He looked at the two Generals. "Thank you, gentlemen. You may be seated." He then stepped one direction, and then the other, appearing to study all of those in attendance.

"The next order of business," he viewed everyone in one quick sweep, "is a cook. If there are two cooks who would like to join us, please let me know."

After a few seconds of silence, a man stood, then the man next to him stood. The first one introduced himself. "My name is Albert Bates. This is my friend Johnny Little. We both know how to cook real good. We cut up that bear, and the meat is drying now."

Alexander was speechless for a moment, then smiled and shook his head. "This is a lucky break. We will send a hunting party out to gather meat and other foods. Give your information to Lex before you leave. Everyone see Lex before you leave. Then, if you can, we could use help clearing trees and building cabins."

Everyone seemed motivated. They formed a line in front of Lex, who logged their information down. The party then shifted to the building site. The cooks, and various women worked together to get a good meal ready for the laborers.

The day was long and hard, but successful. Alexander and Kibble talked for a while with a large group of men about weapons and discipline.

Order was established, and rank designated. The archers joined together. The swordsmen and spear-men formed groups.

At the end of the day, Kibble and Alexander stood viewing the progress. "This is going to be faster than I thought." Alexander jabbed his sword into the ground and smiled.

CHAPTER THIRTY-THREE

Everyone dug in over the next few months and worked hard. Even through the winter season, work was not impeded. Local Indians taught them a lot about the proper clothing for warmth and durability.

Cabins were all up, and the wall nearly complete around the town. Making the wall was a huge project, with the circumference reaching one mile.

The townspeople worked well with the Spanish speaking group. Alexander relayed information as needed.

Two cabins sat close to the gate. One was occupied by the professor, Derek, and Alexander. The other housed James and Lex, who had found their compatibility to be very good.

This had led to a wedding ceremony.

Alexander worked out a schedule to rotate between construction and military drills. It had worked well, and the men were gaining skills in both archery and spears. The automatic weapons squad was still in place as a kind of special ops unit. The helicopter, of course, was the ultimate weapon, and Alexander reserved the right to use it at any time he deemed necessary.

At cabinet meetings it was decided that the helicopter must be close by at all times. It was not only important for protection, but as a recruiting tool as well.

The time was nearing to go out on that first recruiting trip. With good weather on the horizon, they would head north, and see how far they could spread their influence.

The final meeting before the trip was in session. The location was a conference room in the home of Alexander. Seated around a finely crafted wooden table were the cabinet members, along with the two generals...Jens Brock and Richard Dickie.

Alexander leaned forward in his chair, fidgeting with his sword, as he frequently did. Suddenly, like lightening, he drew out the sword and raised it straight into the air. His white teeth shown as he exclaimed, "Onward to victory!"

Those around the table were unsure how to react, but at the same time, they had come to know Alexander and his mannerisms. He lowered the sword, and just as quickly, thrust it back into the sheath. He looked around the table before he spoke. "When I say victory, I don't mean that we will attack without cause. What I mean is that our plans will succeed. Our influence will spread, our numbers will increase, and our power will grow."

Without much pause, he blurted out a question. "General Dickie, do you or General Brock know how far north is the next settlement."

Dickie diverted to Jens with a shrug of the shoulders. "I can tell you that Jens knows that area much better than I."

Jens nodded. "Going north is the right direction to meet a lot of settlers. But they do have to fight Indians constantly. Don't know why. They are just on the war path over there." Jens looked at Alexander. "The settlers are fierce fighters, but the Indians are too many. They are loosing the war. I think if you were to help them deal with the Indians, they would join with you."

Alexander turned his head and gazed into nowhere, one hand on his sword. Fire leaped from his eyes as he pounded his fist on the table. "This is perfect!" He exclaimed. "We have to take advantage of this opportunity. We will finish the wall tomorrow and travel north the next morning."

He turned his attention to Derek. "We will need the helicopter to stay pretty close to the group. Use your own discretion. Carry guns and ammunition."

Looking at James and Lex, he continued. "You know we will need as many medical supplies as you can find. And travel close to the rear for easier access."

"We should clear something up." Kibble voiced a concern. "I assume the families will be staying, so we'll have to leave a contingent of soldiers here to protect the fort and those staying behind."

"Good point." Alexander agreed. "Our total force is 140 men. We should leave 40 of them here."

Kibble offered another thought. "Our main purpose is to build the army. In that case, if it's possible that we'll need to travel long distances, we should tell the families so they can plan."

Alexander agreed. "The generals will see to that. As far as how long we will be gone...this initial trip should not be very extended. We just can't say for sure."

After ironing out some ancillary details, Alexander ended the meeting. Plans were set for their first campaign in the New World.

CHAPTER THIRTY-FOUR

The wall did get finished the next day. There was no way for an enemy to get into the town except through the gates.

A platform was made for guards to walk and see over the wall along the entire circumference.

One hundred men marched away the next morning headed north. Being ¼ mile from the sea, they were sure to run into any settlers along the coast.

Jens knew exactly where the largest population was...the one engaged in conflict with the Indians. But there were some smaller settlements along the way.

The leaders traveled together at the front, followed by the army, with Lex and James at the tail. Derek stayed with the chopper, planning to wait 30 minutes, then fly to another landing site near the army.

Alexander's European group of 30 men were carrying guns. This group was called Regiment A, under his direction. The townspeople numbered 70, and were called Regiment B.

Knowing there were hostile Indians ahead, Alexander insisted everyone be in top form. The army traveled through sparse jungle, making good time for two hours, with Derek keeping pace at regular intervals.

Upon reaching the crest of a hill, Alexander could suddenly see a small township. Dwellings were crudely constructed as though not permanent. People were busily scurrying about, as though something was happening.

Alexander raised his arm, halting the army behind him. Jens came forward. "These are settlers from England, but the large town is still an hour ahead.

Alexander rubbed his chin in thought. "There is something wrong down there. You and Kibble come with me. Dickie, you are in charge here, but watch for my signal to approach."

The three men slowly made their way down the hill. As they came into the clearing, two men with swords at their waist approached them. Both were burly and bearded, also carrying bows and arrows over their shoulders. One held up his hand and spoke. "Who are you, and what is your business?"

Alexander, Kibble, and Jens stood side by side, each carrying an automatic weapon. Alexander answered the question. "We are your friends. We came from a settlement two hours south of here. I am Alexander, and I have 100 armed men at the top of the hill."

The two men glanced up at the hill and hesitated slightly. Then the spokesman softened his tone. "Well, then you are welcome here. I am Teddy Jenkins, and I'm in charge. We have 50 men. You should not be traveling this way unless you are prepared to fight Indians."

"That is why we are here." Alexander replied. "You look like you may be going somewhere."

Teddy stood up straight, squeezing his bow with one hand. "We're moving north to Grangetown. They never bothered us before, but lately we've had raids constantly."

Alexander made good eye contact. "We are going north as well, and when we finish with these Indians, you can choose to live wherever you want."

Teddy narrowed his eyes. "That sounds a bit cocky. Are you sure you know what you are talking about?"

Alexander smirked as he glanced at Kibble. Raising his gun and taking aim at a nearby bank of trees, he blasted them out of sight with rapid fire. He nonchalantly lowered the weapon and looked at Teddy. "They will not have a chance."

Teddy scrutinized the gun. "I've never seen the likes of that. Where did you get such a weapon?"

Alexander explained. "This gun is from the future, as well as Mr. Kibble, here. I am from the past. But we can talk later. Now we should get moving."

Teddy's eyebrows raised, while his sidekick shook his head in disbelief.

Alexander turned and gave the signal for the army to approach. As they moved down the hill, a noise pierced the sky overhead. It was Derek and the chopper, staying within close proximity. He descended for a landing in the clearing.

Teddy and his friend appeared to have seen a ghost.

They scrambled to the nearest tree and crouched down like scared rabbits.

Kibble and Jens resisted an urge to break out in laughter, but Alexander threw back his head and bellowed...struck with irresistible hilarity. The two buff men cowering under the branches was too much for him.

The noise overwhelmed everything until Derek landed and powered down.

When they saw Derek get out of the aircraft and walk toward the group, the two men looked at one another and began crawling out from under the tree.

Alexander gathered the leaders together and awaited their arrival. With ashen faces, they approached. Before arriving, Teddy's sidekick bolted and ran, with no explanation.

CHAPTER THIRY-FIVE

Teddy stood in the circle bravely, bearing a shocked and astounded appearance. Alexander took a center position, capturing the attention of all.

He focused on the newcomer. "Teddy, as I said, we have people and technology from the future. We have weapons powerful enough to defeat anyone. We are not afraid of these Indians, or the ones in Grangetown. Now, I ask you, will you be traveling with us?"

Teddy shuffled his feet and scanned the circle, ending up at Alexander. "I would be foolish not to accept your offer. Yes! Indeed we will!"

Within 30 minutes Teddy's town was ready to go, including 50 fighting men and 75 women and children. That brought the army's numbers to 190 men.

The journey to Grangetown was uneventful, and the trail was straight and level. As the army approached, however, a great commotion could be heard. Alexander knew that sound very well. He turned around and issued orders. "The town is under attack! I want men with guns forward, and all others following. Shoot to kill only if necessary. We may be able to scare them away."

Alexander led the way. "Let's go!" He yelled, waving his hand. The guns led the way, including Kibble, who did his best to keep up. The trail widened, leading into town. They ran along the bottom of the wall, but could see that it was unfinished.

The sounds of battle grew louder until at the end of the wall, the scene opened up to them.

Many people were lying motionless on the ground. The settlers were being driven back by large numbers of Indians armed with bow & arrows, spears, and dart blow pipes.

Alexander led the group to a point he deemed good to make a stand. He raised his gun and opened up on the advancing warriors. The others followed suit. It took no more than a few seconds for the tribe to realize things were working against them. They began to fall back, and then as panic set in, they broke into a running retreat.

The Grangetown settlers cheered...wildly pumping their fists into the air.

Then, from the south, came an ear-spitting noise, as Derek maneuvered the helicopter over the treetops. He saw what was taking place, and decided to follow the retreat to make sure there would be no regrouping. He flew over their heads to incite hysteria. After completing a sweep, he estimated there were 500 Indians.

He flew up and around so he could come in from behind again. Gliding low over their heads, he plastered trees with machine gun fire. The men dropped all weapons and scrambled for cover.

Derek looped around again and fired a missile into a nearby hillside. The blast sent them out of their minds. Like scared rabbits, they were fleeing toward home as fast as they could go.

Derek backed off and hovered to one side. His plan was to follow them to their village. As he coasted along, the direction of their retreat became clear...west. Patiently lurking in the shadows for 30 minutes, he finally saw them reach their village.

As the befuddled warriors poured into their safe haven, Derek revved it up for one final mock attack. The chopper came bellowing into the village with guns blazing at the nearby trees.

A full fledged panic resulted. Men, women, and children blitzed down a western bound trail at top speed. Derek estimated their numbers at about 2,000. He hung around pestering them until they were well on their way down the trail. As he turned and headed back, he was pretty sure no one would be attacked by them again.

Back at Grangetown, James and Lex had their hands full tending to the wounded. Of the settlers, 25 were wounded,

20 dead. Of the Indians, 30 dead, no survivors.

Their time was mostly taken up digging out arrowheads and dressing wounds. James was also able to function as Reverend Jacobs to grieving families.

Alexander gathered the leaders together for a meeting just as Derek was landing. Two logs served as seating for the group. Discussion opened as Derek arrived and took a seat.

"Now we will get news of the enemy." He eyed Derek, who was happy to respond. "I doubt we'll see them again. At last look, they were running down a trail going west. I'd say about 2,000 of them."

Alexander stood and paced between the logs for a moment. He then turned around, searching out Eric Sams. "Mr. Sams," he began. "I have two questions for you." Eric sat up straight, smiling. "Anything, seeing as how you just did save our lives."

Alexander nodded and continued. "Would any of your men be willing to join us in our quest for safety and order?"

"Ha!" Eric started thrusting his fist straight up. "I'm sure that most of Grangetown will join, including me. We have about 500 fighting men right now."

"Spectacular!" Alexander barked, as he pulled his sword, hurling it up in the air. He caught it and slammed the blade into the ground. The blade was still quivering as he continued. "Second question. How far is the next settlement, and are there any hostiles up the coastline?"

Eric stood to speak, scanning the whole group, stopping at Alexander. "The answer is yes, there is a large settlement ten miles north of here. I don't know much about them, but I can tell you there is a great tribe of hostiles between here and there."

"Has there been any fighting?" Alexander queried. "Yes." Eric was emphatic. "A lot. The natives are fierce...that's all I know."

"Very good, Mr. Sams." Alexander paced...hands behind his back. "This is what we will do." He announced.

"Go back to the fort and regroup. In a few days we will come back here to say hello to the hostiles."

CHAPTER THIRTY-SIX

After burying the dead and resting a while, the army from the fort started the three hour trek back home. Teddy Jenkins, the small settlement leader, stayed with Eric Sams and the Grangetown group.

Alexander made an appointment to meet up at this very spot in two days to blaze a trail north through hostile territory.

On the way back, Kibble talked with Alexander, Lex, and James about a trip to 2026, and another test of the direction of the future. It was decided to make this visit the next day, after fueling and maintenance of the chopper.

Everyone was exhausted that night, and turned in early.

The next day Alexander told the generals to find out who really needed to stay home, and who was up for a more lengthy sojourn the next day.

The five time travelers met in the men's cabin to discuss their next move. Kibble led the discussion. "I know we haven't progressed very far with our reform, but it pays to keep tabs on how the changes will affect the future."

Lex quickly spoke up. "I am in full agreement. Sure, we have to make reforms, but I really want to get back to a modern life style. I don't want to miss a chance to get back to a good future."

James smiled and offered a response to his wife's statement. "Of course, I came from an intolerable future. I don't know what a good one would be like, but I'm certainly willing to help get us there."

"It will be interesting," Derek jumped in, "to see just what our efforts have done to affect the future. If we can detect any changes for the better, it will be encouraging."

"On a tactical note," Kibble added, "I think we should stay on the ground during transport. The last two times we've had close calls with getting shot during flight."

"Certainly we should be as safe as possible." Alexander reacted with a confident nod of his head. "My goal is to improve the world we are living in now. If we do that, the future will take care of itself. But I do understand your need to check our progress."

Kibble looked around the table. "Well, I believe we are ready. Just remember to keep your weapons handy. Let's get under way."

A few minutes later everyone was strapped in except James, who volunteered once again to secure himself between two seats.

Derek punched in the data for 2026, and their present location in modern-day North Carolina.

In a flash, the spinning and whirring sound began.

Everyone sat motionless, but the vibration and noise carried on for two minutes, followed by the loud bang. As the noise dissipated, voices burst through from outside.

Derek sensed danger, and quickly started typing in the return trip. Suddenly the door burst open, and six gun barrels were thrust into the faces of Alexander and Kibble.

"Drop your weapons and step outside!" An order was shouted into the cockpit. Derek's hands froze. Kibble and Alexander looked at each other. They slowly put their guns on the floor and unbuckled their belts. Hands raised, they moved out the door and onto the pavement.

The captors at once gruffly barked out commands. "Get on the ground!" They shoved the two men to the pavement. At this moment their backs were turned to the chopper.

To Derek's horror, he discovered that he had accidentally pushed the go switch. Their return trip was commencing. He swiftly jumped out of his seat and pulled the door shut, latching it.

Whirring and spinning began in earnest. Lex gasped and James gripped the seats. Derek knew it would take a couple minutes to complete the time travel sequence.

Concerned that they might storm the cockpit, he pushed the ignition and started the engine. Somehow the return sequence stopped at this point. The soldiers tried to open the door. They shook the handle, kicking and pounding intermittently.

Fearing that shots would be fired next, Derek lifted off, gathering speed as fast as possible. The gunfire did come next, bouncing off the solid hull as the chopper escaped into the sky.

CHAPTER THIRY-SEVEN

From prone positions, Kibble and Alexander strained their necks to see the chopper under fire, speeding away, and then suddenly vanishing from sight. Both knew that they had safely escaped.

For a fleeting moment, Kibble wondered if Derek would go back in time to just before their departure. Thus, he could avoid this disaster. However, Kibble and Alexander would still be stuck in this particular time thread, while other versions of themselves would go on to succeed.

The professor shook his head in bewilderment. This was blowing his mind.

"OK, stand up, now!" The order rang out. Alexander and Kibble slowly regained their feet. Hand cuffs were applied to both before being led away. Down a long sidewalk they went, which led to a huge four story building. The bars on all the windows told the story...this was a prison. Up two flights of stairs they went, and into an office. The two men were ushered to the front of a big desk where a bald man sat. Dangling down his face was a thick handle bar mustache.

He took one look at the prisoners and raised one hand to the guards. "Take the cuffs off."

At once, two of the four guards stepped forward and unlocked the handcuffs.

"Now." The man barked, as he leaned back in his chair. "You men were seen under some unusual circumstances." He suddenly lurched forward in his chair, resting his elbows on the desk. "I wish you would tell me about it." His beady eyes rested on Kibble, then switched to Alexander.

"My apologies!" He blurted out. "First things first. My name is Warden Black. What I say around here goes. My word is the law! So now, who are you, and where did you come from?"

After a few seconds of silence, Kibble answered. "I am professor Kibble, and I am a time traveler. I came from the same year as you: 2026, but from a world parallel to your own."

Warden Black squinted his eyes and screwed up his nose. He just stared at Kibble, as if deciding whether to believe him or not. "Hmm. They said you came out of a strange looking aircraft, and that it disappeared in flight."

He rubbed his chin, and his eyes turned onto Alexander. "And who are you?" Alexander raised his head high.

Standing erect, he answered. "I am Alexander the 3rd of Macedon. You may know me as Alexander the Great."

The warden's eyes widened. He pushed out from behind the desk and stood up. Stepping over to Alexander, he studied his face. Placing his hands on his hips, he began muttering. "Deep set dark eyes, heavy brow, dark curly hair."

He backed up a step, still in thought. Raising one finger into the air, he nodded. "You know, they say when Alexander the Great conquered Europe, there was a mysterious flying machine that went up against his enemies, causing panic."

Alexander and Kibble made fleeting eye contact.

The warden continued. "Did you know that you have been a great hero for over 2300 years? I don't think anyone ever thought that you may be a time traveler, but it all makes sense now."

Alexander looked down, shuffled his feet, and cleared his throat. "I am very glad that you are a student of history. I hope you realize that we are not here to cause any trouble."

The warden chuckled. "You are correct about that. I am not just a history student. I'm a fanatical history student." He turned and spoke to the guards. "All of you wait outside the door."

The four guards immediately complied, closing the door and standing outside.

He looked at Alexander. "I am prepared to cut a deal with you gentlemen. I'll set you up here real nice until your people come after you. But when they do, I go along."

The two prisoners glanced at one another. Alexander wasted no time. "Sir, you have a deal. Can you be ready at a moment's notice?"

"Yes, any time!" The warden was emphatic. "Here, let me give you something." He turned and opened a desk drawer. "Wear these name tags at all times. You can go anywhere and people will see that you are auditors. They won't bother you." He stepped away again, opening a closet door. Disappearing for a moment, he re-emerged carrying a stack of clothes.

"Put these on to make you look at home here. There's one more thing. He opened another desk drawer, pulling out two items. Handing one to each man, he explained. "These are communicators. I have mine on 24 hours a day. Call me anytime and I'll be there in no more than five minutes."

He reached into the top drawer once again and grabbed a key, handing it to Alexander. "This is your room key. It's number 2. My room is number 1, and they're both on the first floor. Go to meals in the cafeteria for free."

He turned up his palms. "Can I be any clearer, gentlemen? I want to go with you. I don't like the world I live in. Don't leave without me."

Kibble held out his right hand. As they shook, he replied. "Warden Black, you have my word."

Turning to leave, Alexander hesitated. "Please, would you tell your men not to shoot if an aircraft shows up for us?"

The warden laughed. "Good point. I'll have it done."

CHAPTER THIRTY-EIGHT

On the way down to the first floor, Alexander posed a question. "Do you think Derek will attempt some kind of rescue?"

Kibble replied with no hesitation. "It's not a matter of 'if', it's a matter of 'when'. The boy's a genius. He will figure it out."

Alexander and Kibble took a little time for themselves.

After a good meal in the cafeteria, they did some laundry.

Sitting at a small table in their room, Kibble was doing some calculations with pencil and paper. Finally he slapped the pencil down and looked at Alexander. "I've come to the conclusion that he can't find our location without great risk to himself. We can make it a lot easier for him if we spend as much time outside as possible."

Alexander rested a foot on a knee while drumming his fingers on the table. A purse-lipped smile came over his face. "Well, I guess we have spent enough time in here, then. We should go to the place where we last saw him."

Kibble nodded in agreement, while he stood, placing the pencil and paper into the front pocket of his new coveralls.

Looking very workman like, they both went out the door and down the hallway. As they exited the building, Kibble did a double take of someone sitting in a lobby chair. He thrust his arm out to grab Alexander, who was all the way out the door. Both men stepped back into the building, and stared at the man in the chair. It was Derek, dressed in the same crisp coveralls, and staring back at them.

They gravitated from the doorway to the chair, blinking their eyes in disbelief. Kibble shrugged his shoulders and raised his eyebrows. His lips attempted to form a word, but Derek responded first. "I knew you were in this building."

Alexander asked the obvious question. "Where did you get that suit?"

Derek laughed. "Just know this. You can do anything with mathematics."

Kibble then came out with the next most pressing question. "So where is the helicopter?"

Derek stood and checked his watch. "I programmed the doormac for James. In 30 minutes he's going to show up on the pavement."

Alexander shook his head in amazement. "You are unbelievable." He smiled as he grabbed the communicator from his pocket. "We need to contact the warden now."

Derek looked puzzled. Kibble laughed. "It's OK. He wants to go back with us."

A voice blared from the two communicators in their possession. "Alexander! What's going on?"

Alexander pressed the talk button. "We are at the front door. Can you meet us very soon for the trip?"

The warden's voice carried overtones of excitement. "Splendid! I'll be right there!"

Derek still wasn't convinced. "How do you know he isn't trying to trick you? I wouldn't trust him."

Kibble smiled. "We had a conversation with him. He seemed as genuine as James did."

Within five minutes warden Black came shuffling up to the lobby carrying a backpack. The three men stood to meet him. Kibble made the introduction. "This is Derek, my assistant, and inventor of the time machine."

The warden shook Derek's hand. "That's pretty impressive. A boy your age mastering time travel. By the way, you can call me Jerry. The sooner I can lose my present identity, and get out of this world, the better."

"You are about to get your wish." Derek replied. "We have 15 minutes before our ride shows up, so we should move out."

"And don't worry." Jerry reassured. "I gave strict orders not to fire on any aircraft."

Derek led the way to the parking lot. After five minutes of walking, they arrived at the exact location. "He'll materialize right here." He pointed to the spot. "We need to stand back about 20 feet."

As the group tarried for ten minutes, waiting for James' return, Jerry peppered them with questions. "So where are we going from here?" He asked.

Alexander piped up. "To 16th century America. Our goal is to build an empire that is secure and strong, but still based on equality and fairness for every individual."

Jerry appeared to be impressed. Eyebrows raised and head nodding, he replied. "That certainly would be opposite of what we have here."

"The aircraft you will see is called a helicopter." Kibble volunteered. "The time machine is inside the helicopter.

After we're all buckled into our seats, the time machine will be started. Don't be afraid when the spinning and whirring noise starts."

Just as Kibble's words trailed off, a boom sounded, and the chopper appeared in front of them.

CHAPTER THIRTY-NINE

An ashen faced James swung the door open and then sat in a passenger seat. He spoke to Derek, who got into the driver's seat. "It's a miracle I made it back here."

Derek laughed "I had confidence in you."

Kibble jumped in quickly. "Buckle up fast. We should leave soon as possible."

Derek programmed the trip back and hit the switch.

Jerry sat wide-eyed, inspecting everything like a child with a new toy. "Goodby, and good riddance to this place." He declared, as the whirring and stirring commenced.

When the final boom sounded, the group breathed a collective sigh of relief, and unloaded.

Alexander directed Jerry toward the cabin. "Welcome to the year 1500." He said with a grin. "Let us have a seat inside."

As the two men made themselves comfortable, Alexander spoke. "I know you have many organizational and leadership skills. I am hoping you will help me to run a government."

Jerry nodded and returned a smile. "I heard you say something about fairness and freedom. That's the kind of work I would be interested in being a part of."

Alexander seemed pleased. "We are about to march into hostile Indian territory tomorrow. Why don't you come along and see what you think?"

That night Alexander met with everyone in preparation for the lengthy campaign.

Discussion topics were: estimated trip length, personnel, formations, and any questions.

No time limit was given for the journey. In fact, he stated that the main army may never return, but some may be sent home, and be replaced by others from the same location. It was understood that some family men would not want endless travel, and these would be permanently stationed at towns scattered along the coast.

There would be no cruel and unfair hierarchy. Anyone would be allowed open dialog with Alexander and the cabinet at any time.

By day's end, everyone knew whether they were going, and what they would be doing.

In the cabin, Jerry shared space with Alexander, Kibble, and Derek. All slept well in preparation for a lengthy and exciting journey, campaign, and quest.

At the appointed time the next morning, 150 men stood in formation, as Alexander briefed them before the journey.

His words and tone inspired the men to do just about anything he asked. They were anxious to begin the mission, and stay as long as it took to complete it.

The cabinet were all present, of course. It's members now included Alexander, Kibble, Derek, James, Lex, and Jerry. It was apparent to the time travelers that they could not yet return to the future. Much more work must be done before future travel would be safe and happy. They were now all committed to forming a stable society, no matter how long it took.

A small command of those who wished to stay was left at the fort, numbering 50 men. The three hour trek to Grange-town was uneventful. The former small township was vacant with no signs of occupation. But at Grange-town, the group of 550 men were awaiting their arrival: 50 from the township, and 500 from Grange-town.

While they waited, this group had been gathering and storing food of all kinds. This was turned over to the head cooks: Albert Bates and Johnny Little.

Alexander took some time to place his total of 700 men under two commands. One under General Brock, and the other under General Dickie.

Before starting into hostile territory, Alexander talked with Derek about avoiding casualties on both sides by using the helicopter to scare them away, thus avoiding conflict. The main goal was to make friends and allies with everyone. Having to kill anyone would make it much more difficult.

Alexander headed north along the coast, making no attempt to disguise the army's location. He and Regiment A took the lead. He had no information to go on except the report of very hostile natives in this area.

The men traveled on edge, expecting company at any time. Within an hour he encountered a sheer rock wall that elevated about 50 feet from where he stood. On the right was a steep decline consisting of jagged rocks that wound up to the top of the cliff.

Approaching the front, and stepping up to Alexander, was Eric Sams, the Grange-town leader. He pointed at the trail. "This leads to the fiercest of the tribes. Their dwelling is at the top of this cliff. I would be well prepared to encounter them, because they always attack on sight. We've never been able to accomplish any kind of communication with them."

Alexander scanned the ocean, cliff, and trail. "We must go up the trail." He replied. "This looks like a job for Derek and the helicopter." He took a few steps up the trail.

"But I really don't like just going after them without giving them a chance first to talk with us."

He turned and looked at Eric. "I'm going to take Regiment A up with me. The rest will follow after us. When Derek arrives, we may need his help, but let us try this first."

The two generals stood there taking note. Alexander signaled Regiment A to follow, and they started up the trail.

CHAPTER FOURTY

Alexander remained in the lead as the narrow trail twisted and turned, finally reaching the top of the bluff.

Seeing flat open space for 100 yards, he emerged onto the bluff, followed by Regiment A and the entire 700 men.

Leading the army forward, he could see that the bluff continued on indefinitely. There was only ocean to the right, and a distant forest to the left.

Halting, he turned and gave word for everyone to march four abreast. Soon his men were all on the bluff, maintaining high alert.

As Alexander scanned the forest, he began to see movement. All along the trees were men emerging...an entire army walking toward them. He immediately halted and gave orders for a left face. He informed Regiment A to take out smoke grenades, and await the order to throw them.

All along the line, the archers, spear-men, and swordsmen were on battle alert.

Alexander just waited, watching Indians pour out of the forest. Soon he realized that their numbers were great, approaching 5,000. Still, he didn't flinch, and appeared to have supreme confidence.

Their front line drew within 50 yards, then 40, then 30. They didn't slow down, but kept coming. At this point he saw archers reaching for their arrows. He saw blowpipes elevating to mouths, and tomahawks rising for the attack.

Turning to Regiment A, he barked out the order to throw the smoke grenades. The men tossed them just in front of the approaching line, about 20 yards. Suddenly, thick, black smoke belched into the air, totally obscuring vision.

Alexander ordered guns raised in case the smoke was not a deterrent. But as Regiment A stood in readiness, no one was breaking through the smoke. Alexander's arm remained frozen in mid air. He stood like a statue for 2 minutes. Nothing happened.

Eternity progressed to five minutes, and the smoke began clearing. The Indian front line had halted in apparent bewilderment of the smoke. Guns were still raised, and weapons on the other side were primed as well.

One Indian, who appeared to be the chief, yelled out an order. Everyone on the front line raised tomahawks high into the air, as if readying for a surge attack.

Quickly, Alexander shouted, "Shoot the weapons out of their hands!" Regiment A instantly followed the order. The raised tomahawks were obliterated by gunfire. The Indians looked around in shock, wondering what had just happened.

Still determined, the chief ordered everyone to attack.

He jumped and waved his arms wildly, as if throwing a tantrum. The front line grabbed knives from their belts, and lurched forward, yelling and screaming.

Alexander then issued another order. "Fire at the ground in front of them!" Regiment A complied, sending dirt and rocks flying directly in front of their feet. They did some high-step dancing in an attempt to avoid these strangely effective weapons.

The chief was beside himself. Running back and forth, he hollered loudly at his men to continue the attack.

Regiment A ceased firing, but the Indians did not attempt to advance. The chief continued his tirade, but the front line stayed where they were.

At that moment came a loud noise from above. Derek and the chopper had arrived. He came in low, swooping directly above the Indian front lines and began descending closer to the ground.

They took one look above their heads, and immediately dropped their weapons, running at top speed back to where they came from.

Derek circled around to face their retreat, hovering above the now empty space that the tribesmen had just vacated. He descended slowly, and softly landed.

CHAPTER FOURTY-ONE

Derek stepped out of the chopper and joined the gazing party. Alexander intently watched the tribal retreat. It appeared they were going to dissipate into the forest, but a small contingent remained just at the edge. The Indians watched as though curiosity had overcome fear.

Alexander approached Kibble and the generals. He folded his arms in thought. "I would like to talk with the chief." He began. "If there is a chance to have dialogue, I should try to do it."

Kibble showed some apprehension. "I think we should bring some protection with us. They seem pretty wild to me."

Alexander nodded. "Regiment A will be close by, but we must go out and offer to speak with them by ourselves."

He turned to the generals. "Jens and Richard, you will follow us and stay back a few paces. We are ready. Let us proceed." He turned to Regiment A, and spoke in Spanish. "Be ready to approach if there is any trouble." Waving quickly to Warden Black, he motioned with his head. "Jerry, come with us." He, Jerry, and Kibble then began walking, followed a few paces behind by Jens and Richard.

Alexander estimated the tree line to be 200 yards away.

As the three of them walked side by side, he carefully eyed the Indians. He saw two of them quickly turn and duck back into the forest.

He managed his pace to a slow, but steady advance.

Momentarily, the two Indians re-emerged, followed by a highly decorated man who was not the same chief he saw on the battle field.

The men soon reached 100 yards, and Alexander kept walking. He could see there was a buzz among those who surrounded the chief. They were having a spirited conversation, and some exhibited highly animated behavior. But the chief responded with firm gestures. He seemed to be confident and decisive, making up his own mind about their topic of discussion.

At about the 30 yard mark, Alexander halted and just stood there, with his two companions following suit. He said nothing, but keenly watched the natives' every move. The chief's body language did not seem to indicate aggressive action, but Alexander, nonetheless, maintained a grip on his gun. Then the chief stepped forward and started walking straight toward them. He was joined by one man on each side.

Alexander did not move, but held his ground, allowing the chief freedom to act as he wished. He appreciated the confident air about this man, which seemed to match his own style.

As the Indian party drew closer, he saw new details.

The chief's face was covered with paint. His hair hung long over his shoulders, but part of it was rolled up at the top with long sticks poked through in several directions. Eagle claws dangled down his deer skinned top.

All three Indians held spears and carried bows and arrows. Knives were attached to their waistlines. So no one trusted the other, but both parties were willing to talk.

Alexander knew that this was a positive sign. He noticed right away that the chief conducted himself with supreme confidence. He held his chin high, showing a relaxed and fearless manner.

Alexander almost felt that he had known and valued his friendship before. He was pretty sure that the chief was the reason the entire tribe was not still running through the forest in retreat.

The chief then held out both arms, with palms up, and began to speak. His language, though in Shawnee, held a familiar ring to Alexander. He quickly thought back to some of the ancient languages he had studied in his youth. He realized there must be some connection between Asia and the American natives.

He found himself comprehending many of the chief's words. "You... fight...not like...white men. You have weapons...too strong. You have...giant bird. Shawnee want...be your friend."

Alexander responded quickly, summoning the familiar language that he had learned so long ago. "We do have powerful weapons. No one can defeat us, but we would like to be your friends. We do not want to fight you."

The chief was visibly moved at this man's ability to speak his language. He stepped forward slightly, looking at Alexander. "I am Young Eagle, chief of the Shawnee. We have always been stronger than anyone, even the Cherokee. What you bring here today, I have never seen. If you do not fight us, we will be your friends. You can pass through our land anytime."

Alexander smiled and nodded slightly. "We really do not want to fight anyone. We want to bring peace everywhere. We thank you for the passage through your land, and we wish to stay for one night. We will leave tomorrow."

The chief turned around and shouted an order to his men standing next to the forest. They cheered and pumped their fists into the air, some of them disappearing into the trees.

The chief faced Alexander again. "We will have big feast here. But first show me...giant bird."

Alexander nearly burst out laughing, but politely held back. He motioned to the chief. "Follow me."

CHAPTER FOURTY-TWO

The day went well. Chief Young Eagle was even given a ride in the chopper. He was visibly shaken, but thrilled flying over the treetops and above his village.

The two camps combined food for the feast. It seemed like an extra large and extra early original Thanksgiving to kibble, Derek, and Lex. There was good will and celebration on both sides.

Alexander talked with the chief for quite a while, gleaning information about nearby tribes and settlements. He also brought up his plan for a unified government. This didn't fit into the chief's world very well. He couldn't get past a tribal concept. The Indians didn't appear to be the kind of people that would fit into his regimental military philosophy.

Kibble and Alexander were happy that no loss of life occurred during that dangerous initial contact. Everyone went to bed feeling good about the day.

The leadership were up early to discuss what their next move would be. The group sat around a campfire, as Alexander made an opening statement.

"Yesterday was a great accomplishment, but today we start a new quest. We will not rest until this land is under one rule. The distance is 3,000 miles from north to south, and 3,000 miles from east to west. But tomorrow we start a new goal. A short distance to the north lies another settlement.

We will spend a little time there to set up an outpost and possibly build a fort."

Kibble reacted with some feedback. "It would seem like the best plan to go up and down the coast to establish our presence. Then our influence would naturally flow westward."

Alexander heartily affirmed that. "Our goal is nothing short of that. We head north to the future Canadian border, establishing towns, forts, and armies. Then we backtrack and keep going to Mexico. After we reach that goal, we will decide on the next move."

Alexander's army did reach their goal. Moving north and turning settlements into forts, they arrived at the northern 'border'. Backtracking, they revisited each establishment as they traveled south. Then, moving farther south, they worked their way to the tip of Florida, This massive undertaking took two years by the time they reached the original settlement in North Carolina. Forts and outposts up and down the coast made a great foundation for a push westward.

It was a warm spring day, as the time travelers met in Alexander's cabin. The topic would be the progress they'd made toward the development of a free and fair society.

Kibble, Derek, Lex, and James joined him, as Alexander sat cross-legged. Showing a confident smile, he looked around the table. "I have discussed this with all of you recently, but officially, I think it's time to explore the future. Does anyone have any more discussion about this?"

Kibble was the first to respond. "Well, I think we've done a very good job of laying the groundwork for a solid government. We really need to find out how all of this has changed history."

"I totally agree." Lex was quick to voice her opinion. "It may be that we'll find a society that we can live in comfortably. I've said this before...I'm not fond of a primitive lifestyle."

Derek sat up and looked around. "If we don't have any luck with traveling straight to 2026, we should travel back to certain places and times. For example, the Babylonian palace may send us to a pre-European conquest time. In that case, we wouldn't find a militaristic America."

"That is absolutely true." Kibble vigorously agreed. "I know that certain travel points have an effect on future historical outcomes."

Alexander nodded. "The work that we have done over the last two years should have a positive effect on the future.

We must discover which future that lies in."

"So let's set a time for travel." Kibble directed the group toward a decision. "Would tomorrow morning work for everyone?"

Everyone agreed.

CHAPTER FOURTY-THREE

The next morning the group met at the helicopter, eager for a new adventure. They didn't want to attract attention, so they discretely jumped in and prepared for the trip.

Everyone buckled up with the exception of James, who insisted on letting the others have seats, while he held on between them. Weapons were in hand.

Derek looked back at his passengers. "If everyone's ready, here we go." He started the engine and soon was lifting off. After reaching a good altitude, he issued another announcement. "We're going to 2026 now. Watch for any approaching aircraft."

Most of the group hadn't time traveled in two years, so it was almost like a new experience. The whirring, shaking, and dizziness began, but didn't last long. An explosion sounded, signifying arrival at their destination.

Everyone immediately peered out the windows in search of a new and better world. Right away they could tell a difference from the past trips back to 2026.

Dotting the landscape were residential areas: streets, houses and cars. There were no signs of military or bondage. No aircraft approached them. Everyone sensed a huge change in the society below.

Derek looked at Kibble and Alexander for a reaction. Kibble pointed straight ahead. "Take it to the skyscrapers ahead. Let's find a good place to land."

Derek quickly gained elevation and headed for the city.

Everyone, still wary, kept a sharp watch for any sign of conflict. The skies were clear. The urban area below appeared tidy and orderly.

The chopper skimmed over the tops of the skyscrapers until Derek sited air traffic ahead. The plane appeared to be an airliner just taking off, and headed skyward toward the right.

Kibble peered below. "This is what we want! We can land at this airport."

As Derek began landing maneuvers, Kibble's eye caught a building adjacent to the airport. He tapped Alexander's arm "That's the capital building. Our chances are better there." Alexander nodded in agreement, while Derek quickly changed course.

A few seconds later, the aircraft flew over the building and descended to a huge lawn, street side.

As the chopper touched ground, there was still no sign of opposition, or even security. Alexander unbuckled his seat belt "Turn it off, Derek. We will get out here." Soon silence reigned, and Kibble's belt popped off.

"OK." Alexander spoke while gripping the door knob. "Kibble and I will go out first, and let you know when to follow."

The door swung open and Alexander stepped down, followed by Kibble. The men walked away from the chopper, heading for a nearby sidewalk.

A few people were starting to gather around. Alexander suddenly handed his weapon to Kibble. "Put the guns in the helicopter, quickly." The professor complied without hesitation, realizing that walking around with arms was a bad idea.

They then strolled calmly to the sidewalk, and toward the building. The crowds closed in, but did not appear menacing. Mostly they were curious bystanders.

The two men walked up several stairs to a level area, and turned around. With about a hundred people already at close range, Alexander made a decision to face them. He lifted up both arms, and signaled for all to approach. At this, the crowd pressed in, eagerly awaiting his words. Kibble thought this was odd, considering the bystanders had no idea who they were.

Alexander then began. "Gather around, everyone. You must want to know who we are, and what we are doing here."

As he opened his mouth to continue, a gentleman from the crowd interrupted him.

"We already know who you are, Alexander."

Kibble and Alexander were both dumbstruck at these words. Immediately, another man spoke. "You are Alexander the Great! And you, sir, must be professor Kibble."

The two glanced at one another. Alexander scratched his head. "How is it that you know us?" He offered the question to anyone willing to answer. A tall, slender man in a suit and tie approached. He placed one hand on Alexander's shoulder. "You are more famous than you realize. If you don't mind following me inside, I can explain it to you."

Raising his eyebrows, Alexander nodded. "Very well, then." He and Kibble accompanied the man up one more set of stairs, and through the front doors of the building. Once in, the man led them to a modest office on the first floor. "Please, gentlemen, have a seat." He offered, motioning with an open hand. He then took a seat himself at the desk.

Folding his hands, he smiled and shook his head in a manner of disbelief.

"You see," he began, "you and your party of five are known as the founders of this nation. You and your aircraft with the time machine in it are a big part of every history book. We know the color and shape of this helicopter, which is how we knew it was you. You are even honored as the center point of the biggest holiday of the year. It has been speculated that some day you would travel back to the future and be recognized."

Alexander leaned back in his chair, arms behind his head. Looking at Kibble, he smiled. "Well, we finally succeeded. This appears to be the kind of society we have been looking for." Glancing at the man in the suit, he posed a question. "What kind of government do you have here?"

The man confidently sat up straight and adjusted his tie. "First of all, my name is Reggie Switzer, and I work for the government. This is the United American Republics. The answer to your question is, this is a strong and fair government. You yourself designed it that way."

Alexander folded his arms in thought. He leaned forward, asking another question. "Can I see the man in charge?"

CHAPTER FOURTY-FOUR

Reggie picked up the desk phone and pushed three numbers. "Sir, this is Reggie. I have two visitors here who want to see you. They are top priority." Pause...... "Thank you, sir."

He then hung up the phone and smiled. "He's waiting for you. I'll take you to his office."

At that, he stood up and stepped toward the door. The two men followed him. Into an elevator they went, and up to the 45th floor, which was the top of the building. As the elevator doors opened, security guards stood, awaiting their passage through metal detectors.

The men strolled by unscathed, entering a large corridor. They approached the door to a huge office. More security was stationed outside the door.

Reggie knocked on the door and waited. Within a few seconds the door was opened by another security guard.

Leading the way, Reggie acted like he was comfortable with the surroundings.

As Kibble and Alexander stepped into the room, they saw a big desk where a gray haired man was rising to his feet.

Reggie did the introductions. "Gentlemen, this is our emperor, Dennis Carrigan. And sir, I would like to introduce you to Alexander the Great and professor Kibble."

The emperor flashed a look at Reggie, then back to the visitors. Reggie filled in the blanks. "The helicopter's in the front. It's the right style and color."

Emperor Carrigan seemed tongue-tied. "Forgive me, gentlemen. I'm trying to absorb this." He swiped his forehead with one hand. Turning, he stepped around the big desk, and up to the visitors. He shook hands with both men and pulled up a chair for himself. "Please, have a seat, all of you."

Having seated himself, he eyed Kibble and Alexander. "So, gentlemen, where did you come from?"

Alexander was quick to answer. "Most recently from the year 1502. We are here now to see how well we have affected the development of the future."

A grin came over the emperor's face. He suddenly could see the true authenticity of his guests. There was something in their mannerisms, speech, and dress that convinced him.

"By the way," he mentioned, "please call me Dennis." Resting his eyes on Alexander, he nodded, confirming his own thoughts. "You must be Alexander. Your bearing gives you away."

Alexander smiled pleasantly. "That, I am indeed." "And may I ask you," Dennis went on, "how long are you planning to stay?"

"That depends on whether we are welcome." Alexander answered. "We will stay if we are welcome."

Dennis leaned back in his chair. "Yes, you are most welcome to stay. In fact, I would like to make you an offer." Touching his chest with an open hand, he continued. "I'm 70 years old, and feel the need to retire. However, I have no children...no one to take over for me. Alexander," his eyes burned intensely, "I don't know you personally, but I recognize a great leader when I see one. This country needs you at the helm. Would you consider it?"

Alexander appeared taken by surprise. He was the picture of concentration, his deep set eyes staring out the window. His heavy brow hung low. His dark curly hair connected to his short scruffy beard, which he rubbed in thought.

Suddenly he met Dennis' gaze, assuming an erect posture, even while seated. "You have a need," his face emanated with charm, "that I am well able to fill. Certainly, I will accept your offer."

He turned to Kibble seated next to him. "There is one condition." He said, looking back at Dennis. He rested one hand on Kibble's shoulder. I need the professor as my assistant...and my friends in the helicopter must remain with me."

Dennis smiled and nodded. "That presents no problem." He agreed "This is going to work out to everyone's benefit. Imagine you founding this country, and then ruling it 500 years later!"

He held out his hand to Alexander, and they shook, sealing the deal.

"Now," he smiled, "I would like to do a little time traveling, just for the fun of it."

CHAPTER FORTY-FIVE

The time travelers led Dennis to their helicopter in order to grant him his wish. They found Derek, Lex, and James engaged in conversation with bystanders. Nonetheless, they were happy to see their leaders return.

Alexander spoke as he approached. "These are the other cabinet members. Derek is an excellent pilot and a genius of science. James and Lex are married, and head up the medical and spiritual branches."

Alexander then reversed the introduction. "I would like you to meet Dennis Carrigan, the King of the United American Republics."

Dennis extended his hand in friendship to all. "It is a great privilege to meet you, the founders of our country.

History has recorded your brave campaign for liberty. It has been a huge success story. But in order to ensure that it continues, the right leadership must remain in office. That's why I've asked Alexander to take over, seeing that I am ready to retire."

Derek, Lex, and James threw their fists into the air in celebration. Lex was the first to speak. "This marks the end of a very long, hard journey through time. We've been looking for a fair and civilized society, and we've finally found it."

"That is certainly true." Dennis agreed. "I do hope you all will stay. As for now, I was promised a time journey to somewhere, and back again. I just want to experience it."

"I have a suggestion." James offered. "Lex and I would just like to stay here. Would you mind setting us up with lodging before you go?"

Dennis heartily complied. He spoke with one of his men standing by, then smiled at the couple. "Follow Max, here.

He'll get you situated, and we all will be back again very soon."

Derek climbed into the driver's seat, which cued the others to follow. Dennis was spellbound by the entire scene, but did as he saw Kibble and Alexander do.

"OK," Alexander issued directions to Derek, "it is back to the home fort location at a time soon after we last departed." Our plan is to talk to generals Brock and Dickie, as well as to see if warden Black wants to return with us."

Derek already had it programmed and ready. Kibble leaned over and offered Dennis a brief explanation of the time machine events. The switch was flipped, and the action began.

Dennis tolerated the commotion and events pretty well, and actually seemed to enjoy all the excitement. After the noise subsided, Alexander turned to Dennis with a smile. "Welcome to 1502. This is where our base camp is located.

We will tie up the loose ends here, and return just as soon as possible.

Doors opened, and everyone stepped out to the interior of the fort, not far from their cabin.

Dennis looked up to the sky and took a deep breath. "I've never breathed air this fresh." He sighed.

Alexander placed his hand on Derek's shoulder. "Notify the two generals and the warden that we will meet in my cabin immediately."

"Sure." Derek replied, and scooted off toward the other cabins.

Within 15 minutes they were all seated around the table, including Jens Brock, Richard Dickie, and Jerry Black. With Derek, Kibble, Dennis, and Alexander, the attendance was seven.

"Thank you, gentlemen, for coming." Alexander began. "This is a very important meeting. A lot is going to change as of right now."

The men looked at one another, as Alexander continued. "We have traveled to the year 2026, and have just now returned. Our mission has been successful. We have found the kind of decent and fair society we were looking for." He looked at Dennis. "This man is the leader of that future society. His name is King Dennis Carrigan. His wish is for me to replace him when he retires. This means that I will be leaving here."

"Alarm appeared on the mens' faces, and they all began talking at once. Alexander held up one hand, and silence ensued.

"There will be no problems." He promised. "This is what we will do. General Dickie will replace me. General Brock will be his assistant, but still continue his current duties. You must find and appoint a replacement for general Dickie."

Alexander held up both hands, his glare burning through everyone around the table. "This is something that you must never forget. Your entire lives will be devoted to this goal...constantly building and pushing westward. But always treat everyone equally, with kindness and fairness.

That way this will some day be the greatest nation on earth." Everyone was quiet as he caught the eye of warden Black. "Jerry, I would like to offer you a position in my kingdom, if you wish to come with us."

Jerry wasted no time in answering. "Indeed, sir, that would be a great honor."

Alexander scanned the gathering around him. "Gentlemen, I wish you good fortune. I know that your efforts will bear fruit, for I have seen the future. It has been a privilege to have your allegiance."

CHAPTER FOURTY-SIX

After the meeting, the return party gathered at the helicopter and said goodby to their friends, many of whom they had known for two years. Richard Dickie, the new Emperor, stood resolutely, waving to the greatest man he'd ever known.

They all wondered how they could carry on without him, but deep inside were confident that they would.

The five men arrived safely to 2026 on the front lawn of the capital building. A group of security were there to greet them, as ordered by Dennis.

Warden Black, seeing it all for the first time, was enthralled with the tidiness and order that contrasted the time thread from which he himself originated.

Dennis assigned the security folks to watch the helicopter, while he led the group up to his office. As they filed through his office door, Dennis asked them to be seated, forming a circle. He grabbed a chair and squeezed it in for himself.

As he took a seat, he addressed the group. "This day will go down in history. The elusive team with the time machine has finally arrived, and is here to stay." He focused on Alexander and Kibble. "I know you gentlemen have made the right choice. We are here to discuss your transition to leadership. Yes, you, Alexander will be the king, and can rule any way you like. However, I will show you what I do for one week. That will enable you to approach the job easier in your own way."

"I like your idea," Alexander agreed, "but I want Kibble and Jerry to join us. Kibble will be my assistant. And Jerry will work as a diplomat to other countries."

"Very good!" Dennis exclaimed. "That leaves one more spot to fill. How will Derek fit into this?"

Alexander smiled, holding out a palm to Derek. "Derek, do you have any input here?"

Assuming an erect posture, Derek prepared to answer, but thought for a moment. "I could help the most by doing what I do best...scientific research and experimentation.

Most specifically, time travel."

Alexander nodded. "A man should not waste his talents. I fully agree."

Kibble leaned forward. "And I'm hoping to put in some time there as well, using my strongest talents."

"You may be able to spend most of your time in the lab." Alexander nodded. "Then we need to assign Lex and James to a position. I will talk to them."

Dennis clapped his hands. "Well, it appears that we're headed in the right direction." As he looked from one to the other at everyone, he appeared to be more of a politician than a king. But that was just his way.

"This country may look like a utopia, and I truly believe it is." He pulled his chair back a little. "But I need to warn you that the rest of the world is far from it. About 90 years ago, a dictator named Adolph Hitler took over Europe. He eventually signed a truce with Russia, and now the two countries cooperate. Their allies are the Japanese, who took over the Philippines and much of Asia." Dennis wore a serious expression. He continued more slowly.

"We are the last bastion of good remaining in the world.

That's why we need to stay strong in every way."

Alexander wrinkled his brow. "Let me ask you...how far do your borders extend?"

"From Mexico, a small country above central America, to the north pole. We have always been by far the most powerful country in the world. But now evil is stacking up against us."

He pulled his chair in closer and focused on Alexander. "That's why the timing is perfect for your arrival. We need a man like you who knows how to conquer and control the world."

Alexander gripped the arms of his chair, exhaling slowly. "I have never had a situation that I could not handle. This will be no exception."

Dennis was pleased. "We should start tomorrow morning. We have a lot to cover. And remember, I will always be available for consultation."

He stood and brought the meeting to a close. "Everyone come in at 8am, and we'll get started."

CHAPTER FOURTY-SEVEN

That first week of learning the ropes went fast for Alexander and company. Dennis explained all the policies and hot spots he was dealing with nationally. He also went over international history, including current problems and priorities.

Alexander felt like he was ready to take the reigns. On the last day he did a televised speech, introducing himself to the nation. His initial popularity was at never before achieved heights. His story was seen as magical and providential. Polls showed that the people literally worshiped him.

He was not concerned with all of this, but only with his success as a leader. Dennis went into retirement, but lived nearby, and was available 24 hours a day. Alexander and Kibble sat in the big office contemplating what they had learned during the fast-paced week. Alexander sat behind the desk twirling a pen between two fingers. He then tapped it hard on the desk.

"Something must be done about all the opposition we are encountering." He addressed Kibble. "Certainly our military power is unequaled, but if most of the world unites against us, I think we are in trouble."

Kibble, seated at the other end of the desk, leaned on it with both elbows. "I've always relied on science to remedy my problems. Why don't we do the same thing now?"

Alexander drew a blank. "What exactly do you mean?" "I mean that we have run out of options." Kibble continued. "The weapons that we have are good, but cannot hold off the entire world. What we need is a super weapon or a super defense system."

Kibble tapped the table with one finger. "Back in the United States, I knew several scientists who were working on defense systems, and had made good progress with it. Their technology would render all conventional and nuclear weapons useless. By shooting a sophisticated laser beam at the enemy, all of their weapons systems would be jammed."

Alexander raised his eyebrows. "What chance do we have of getting a defense system like that?"

Kibble smiled. "A good chance. A very good chance. But we will need to travel into the future. I don't think we have time to develop it on our own without help. We will travel 50 years forward to start with, and go further if needed. As a last resort, we can go back to my career in the USA to get information from my contemporaries."

Alexander leaned back in his chair. "We need to hurry.

The situation is grave. You and Derek should go by yourselves. There is a lot for me to do here." He flashed a serious look at Kibble. "Whatever you do, you can't fail."

Derek and kibble consulted and decided to go forward 25 years to see if the United American Republics would still by free and strong. Their hope was to contact the Alexander of the future and get the secret data from him.

With no time to waste, they met at the helicopter, which was locked in a government warehouse. Derek programmed the doormac to send them to the lawn in front of the future capital building. He and Kibble began the journey, as he flipped the switch to engage. The whirring noise started and increased in volume, but suddenly stopped, followed by an alarm sounding.

Derek squinted at the screen, which showed a warning message. "Destination solid matter." He turned to Kibble. "Hmm...they must have expanded the building."

Kibble nodded. "The safest route would be in the air." Derek busied himself on the keyboard for a moment.

"That should do it."

The two men pushed the chopper out the door and reboarded for another try. Starting the engine, Derek took off and zoomed up to above skyscraper level. Once over the capitol building, he hovered. "Second time's the charm." He grinned at the professor.

No sooner did Kibble answer, "Hope so," than Derek flipped the switch and started the adventure. The chopper banged into the future, and it really was obvious to the time travelers. They didn't even recognize the building. It had been completely redone and expanded. Derek headed in for a landing where he knew the front of the building used to be.

As he approached the ground, something seemed out of sorts. A group of uniformed soldiers suddenly started shooting at them. Alarmed, Derek used automatic reflexes. The helicopter was a sitting duck at its descending angle. He quickly fired a rocket at the ground in front of the men, obscuring their view. He then darted up and away. As he sped forward and upward, he saw something on the rooftop that he hadn't seen before...a swastika flag.

CHAPTER FOURTY-EIGHT

Kibble and Derek sat catching their breath at the airfield, their seat belts still on. Kibble inhaled deeply. "Well, now we know the future if we don't do something about it."

Derek smiled as he nodded. "I assume, then, we're activating plan B... to head back to our own time."

"You are correct." Kibble confirmed. "Let's make it a weekday in 2025 when I was working with professor Ed Worth. He was researching weapons jamming, and progressing quite well when he lost his funding. I plan to give it back to him."

Derek programmed the coordinates back to 2025. "Land in your warehouse?"

"Perfect." Kibble tritely replied. Within five minutes, the two were staring out the chopper window inside the warehouse.

Suddenly Derek was alarmed. "This is 2025. You didn't have this chopper then. What if your counterpart came home and found it sitting here?"

Kibble twirled his mustache. "We do have to get out of here now. We'll have to land on top of the university, or...send us to the 3rd floor museum. There's an open spot on the floor there, and it's after hours. Ed Worth always worked late."

Derek had no trouble getting them to the precise location. They found themselves right in the middle of the museum. They sat in silence for a moment. Kibble checked his watch again. "Ed will still be in his lab. Let's go."

Stepping out in the middle of a museum caused echoing off the bare floor and walls. Kibble and Derek shut the chopper doors at the same time, heading toward a nearby exit into the hallway. Kibble led the way, marching confidently down the hall, checking room numbers. Two minutes later, he stopped at one with the name, "Ed Worth" on the window. He looked at Derek and turned the knob. As the door swung open, he scanned the room, spying a head moving at the far end.

He silently shuffled in and onward, followed by Derek.

They glided across the room, pulling up next to professor Worth. He was unaware of their presence, absorbed in studying test tubes.

"Have a word with you?" Kibble's voice quietly broke the silence.

Ed's bushy eyebrows raised while his bald head turned. "Oh, Kibble!" His attention shifted back to the tube he was holding, then his glance bolted back to Kibble. "My, there's something different about you. Where'd you get that shirt?"

"It's a long story. That's why I need to see you now. He motioned. "You remember Derek, my assistant?"

"Of course." He laughed. "I see him every day." His smile dropped into a confused frown. "OK, give it to me.

There's something odd going on."

Kibble moved in closer. "This is the year 2025, correct?" Before Ed could answer, he continued. Derek and I just came from 2026."

Ed stared, the wheels turning in his mind. "Are you telling me you've been time traveling?"

Kibble didn't hesitate. "Yes. You don't realize that we've gone as far back as 60,000BC. Right now we have little time to explain, but let me just tell you this. Next year there will be nuclear war. Derek and I escaped it, barely, but you won't unless you listen to me."

Ed put the tube down and leaned against the table. "I'm all ears." His voice sounded shakey.

"When we left before the nukes, we ended up visiting Alexander the Great. After assisting him with a campaign in Europe, he came with us to 15th century America. We then campaigned for two years and returned to 2026. We found America a beautiful place to live. However, the world united against us. That's where you come in. We must help you finish your weapons shutdown system." He stroked his mustache, sliding one hand over his face. "Ed, you must go back with us. You have to help us."

Ed shook his head in disbelief. "If this is all true, we've got to get out of here. Show me the time machine."

"Great." Kibble replied. "First, gather the most important documents and test items to continue your project."

Ed bent down, pulling a box from under the table. He picked up a notebook and threw it in. He ran around gathering things all over the lab, tossing them in the box.

Within five minutes the box was full.

That should be enough." He said, the anxiety evident. "Can't take the lab with me."

Kibble lay a hand on Ed's shoulder. "Is there anyone you need to come along with you...family members?"

Ed shook his head. "I've got a married son, but I don't think he'd listen to me."

"OK," Kibble reassured him. "We can always come back later to try."

He led the way back to the helicopter. As Ed followed, he still had trouble taking in these events. As he stepped through the museum door, he was shocked at the sight of the big aircraft. "What? How did you get a helicopter in here?"

Kibble laughed as he walked. "The actual time machine is in the chopper, but the transition phase places a magnetic hood over the entire structure. I was amazed when we successfully tested it."

The men boarded and buckled in. "Now you must understand," Kibble briefed his friend, "that we will be traveling to a different time thread, but not changing the date. It will essentially be the same world whose history has been changed by us."

With that, he nodded to Derek, who initiated the journey. Ed had never believed in the possibility of time travel. He had long ago dismissed any hope of a scientific breakthrough. Now he leaned his head back and waited to be thrust into a different time thread.

A few minutes later, a loud bang ripped through the air, followed by bright sunshine.

CHAPTER FOURTY-NINE

Ed squinted through the bright sun at the air field. On the other side he noticed a huge building with roll-up doors.

"Here we are." Kibble said as he opened his door. "This is an aircraft hanger. The attendants will wheel it inside. From here we drive to the lab."

The three climbed out, Ed taking the precious box of notes and test gear.

On the way to the car, Ed immediately sensed a difference between this society and the one he had just left. He knew the United States had many regulations, red tape, and restrictions. He would soon find that this new country had fewer holdups, and things in general went smoother, quicker. This contrast was the result of a well run monarchy, compared to a clogged up democracy.

At the lab Ed was given the tour. Afterward, the three men sat at a table sipping coffee. "So," Kibble began, do you think you have enough to continue experimenting with weapons shutdown?"

Ed sat his cup down. "Kibble, I don't need any more experimentation. The testing is done. This system works."

Kibble was dumbfounded. "I thought they cut funding before you could finish."

Ed shook his head. "Doesn't that show you how ridiculous the government is? Just give me a day or two, and I'll have it up and running."

Kibble chuckled, flopping back in his chair. "This is going to make our job a lot easier." He sipped his coffee. "We'd better go tell Alexander."

The door to the king's office was opened by the monarch. "Come in, gentlemen." Alexander seemed glad to see them. Once inside, Kibble offered an introduction. "This is an associate of mine, professor Ed Worth."

Alexander shook Ed's hand. "Let's be seated, men." The four of them sat around the table. Alexander appeared anxious. "Our world peace problems are getting worse. I hope you have some solutions for me."

Kibble nodded. "Ed hasn't had time to explain it to me, but he has developed a weapons disabling system."

Alexander pounded the table with his fist, a smile on his face. "This is starting to sound good! Professor Worth, do you mind explaining to us how this works?"

Ed nodded politely, and folded his hands on the table. "Simply put, I have developed a scanner that searches out gun powder and nuclear elements. Once the discovery is made, a disabling system kicks in, shutting down all weapons. They won't be operational until we manually switch off the system."

Kibble posed a question. "How close do you need to be to operate this system?"

Ed chuckled. "Anywhere on earth, provided you have satellites. You do have satellites, don't you?"

"I know they have them." Kibble replied. "I will put you in touch with the right people."

Alexander leaned forward, his bearing radiating with high energy. "Are you saying this will be operational within two days?"

"It should be, yes." Ed answered confidently.

Alexander shoved his chair away from the table and stood. "Gentlemen, do you realize..." he swiftly drew his sword and raised it to the ceiling, "that we are going to rule the entire world?" He whipped his sword through the air a couple of times, then quickly rammed it into its sheath. "Get this done, and disarm their weapons before they can figure out the technology. Do you all know what I mean?"

Heads nodded around the table, and no one dared object.

Kibble and Ed pushed all the right buttons, and within two days, the weapons shutdown system was complete.

Hundreds of hand-held triggers were made. With these, a single assailant could walk up to an army and jam all their guns by simply pulling the trigger and scanning. He could even keep it concealed in his pocket. Nucs and other big weapons could be decommissioned using computers and satellites.

Alexander had key military personnel trained to use the triggers. He set a date to decommission all of Russia's weapons, and coordinate this with landing parties from ships.

It would take four days to train and transport military to fleets off the Russian coast. Meanwhile, the same preparations were being made for Japan, Germany, Iran, India, and South America. Countries would go down one at a time in blitzkrieg fashion. They would know what was coming, but would not be able to stop it. All of this would happen, however, without firing a shot.

On the day scheduled for shutdown, several elite special-ops units were sent to the Russian shore simultaneously, in motorized rafts. By the time they reached land, the big weapons had already been neutralized.

The small units advanced, scanning continuously in every direction to avoid sniper fire. At a certain point, they stopped and waited for large landing parties to join them.

They then advanced, capturing and controlling key cities, and therefore, the entire country. After three days, military headquarters were well established.

At this point, the next phase was started on the Japanese and German shores. After a total of four weeks, the operation was complete.

CHAPTER FIFTY

Alexander kept in contact with all of his allies. Chief among these were the remainder of Europe, China, Australia, and parts of the Philippines. The allies were given assurances that as long as relations remained good, the scanners would not by used on them. But there was no doubt about who was in control.

Three months after the weapons shutdown operation, the cabinet was called to discuss matters of the kingdom.

Those present were warden Jerry Black, Reverend James Jacobs and his wife Lex, Derek, Kibble, Ed, and Alexander as the leader.

Matters were discussed, and decisions made concerning domestic and foreign affairs. Alexander then asked if there were any other items of interest to discuss.

Kibble indicated there was something. "I just want to make all of you aware of this, in case you haven't already thought of it. We do have an opportunity to go back to our original world and take steps to avoid nuclear war." The others looked at one another as though they hadn't thought of this possibility, but no one spoke.

Kibble picked up the slack. "First of all, I wish to be very clear that I love where I am now, and intend to remain here for the rest of my life. But I still would like to snuff out nuclear war, if possible. The question is, would that change the reality that we now experience in this world?"

Derek jumped in. "I don't think so, because we got on course with this world in 1500. The world that went through the nucs was a different time thread."

Alexander leaned forward, showing either a sudden interest, or irritation. "I really think we could save that world, and still preserve the one we have here." He held out his hands. "Both worlds coexist during the same time period.

Why not have peace and harmony in both?"

He stood, drew his sword, and thrust it skyward.

"Another world to conquer! We must reverse this tragedy that has already happened!" Twirling his sword three times, he rammed it into the sheath. "Is everyone in agreement with this? Do we have any objections?" He sat back down in his chair.

Lex now voiced her opinion. "Knowing that there's a nuclear winter going on right now, with people living in caves, and who knows how many are dying of radiation or whatever...if we can go back and change this, we are morally obligated to do so."

"We may have to get tricky," Kibble added, "to convince the government to assist us. But if we show up at a point when nuclear warfare appears imminent, we should be able to get our foot in the door."

Derek brought up a point. "The U.S. government will probably not take over other countries. They should, however, assist us in disabling their weapons."

"Do you remember the day the bombs fell?" Kibble asked. "We'll show up five days before that."

"Of course." Derek assured him. "Nuclear war started on March 18."

"OK," Alexander folded his hands, "we should have four people for this mission. I will go, and Dennis will stand in while I'm gone. Kibble and Derek must go. The last spot must be filled by the weapons shutdown expert."

Ed nodded his approval.

Lex and James were in agreement with everyone going except them.

"Good." Alexander concluded. "We will meet at the air field tomorrow at 8am."

Gathering in a huddle on the blacktop, the foursome conferred while attendants pushed the helicopter out to them.

"First of all, everyone's got a weapons scanner." Kibble passed them out as he briefed them. "As you know, they can be used from your jacket pocket." His speech intensified.

"This is how we are going to use them." He stuffed his own into his pocket. The others followed suit. "Here's the plan. Derek will send us onto the front lawn of the white house.

The date will be March 13, 2026." He paused while everyone fidgeted nervously. "What will we do then? Just wait. You know what's going to happen. In a matter of minutes, we will be surrounded by guns. At this point we will let them have it, keeping the scanners in our pockets. Be sure to scan everything, covering 360 degrees."

Alexander chuckled. "I am getting the picture. When they try to shoot us, and their weapons don't work, we will have a captive audience."

Kibble nodded. "We should then be able to speak to the president, or someone important."

"So we are ready." Alexander seemed anxious to get started.

Kibble offered last minute instructions to Derek. "Transport us to the lawn. Don't start the engine."

Hearts pounded as the men fastened their seat belts and checked the scanners in their pockets. Derek programmed for a couple minutes. "Are we ready?" He called politely.

"Take us out." Alexander issued the order.

The airport crew stood around and watched, as the chopper vibrated, and then disappeared in front of them. A loud popping ripped across the white house lawn, followed by a declining whirring sound. Suddenly a large military helicopter sat on the lawn. A security guard outside the fence heard the commotion and unlocked a nearby gate. His eyes nearly bugged out of his head at the sight of four men climbing out of an aircraft that shouldn't be there. He slammed the gate shut and spread the news over his radio.

The time travelers stood away from the chopper, two in front and two in the rear. As predicted, within two minutes, vehicles and hustle-bustle was heard outside the fence.

Then, the sound of a helicopter came from above.

CHAPTER FIFTY-ONE

"Start scanning!" Kibble softly shouted. The two in front scanned ahead of them, while the two in back scanned behind them. Everyone made sure to include the helicopter that was closing in on them.

"Just so you know," Ed spoke up, "these do scan through solid objects."

The chopper above came lower, then a loud speaker was heard. "Get flat on the ground!"

Kibble called out loud. "Scan the chopper again! He pulled the scanner out of his pocket, aiming it skyward. The others saw and copied his actions.

The scanners were silent, and no weapons sounds were heard. They saw the chopper wobble a bit, then move up and away. It was a good indication that it had tried to fire at them, but then was afraid of being fired upon itself.

"OK!" Kibble ordered. "Scan all around again!" They all did a 360 once, avoiding their own aircraft. Suddenly the gate was kicked open, and soldiers poured through, pointing guns and attempting to fire them.

The soldiers had confused looks on their faces. They all were checking their guns and looking at each other. More soldiers poured through the gate. The time travelers quickly scanned the newcomers, after which the soldiers aimed and squeezed, but couldn't fire.

Alexander stepped forward and raised his hand, as if to offer dialogue. He advanced further, and continued walking until he reached the line of soldiers. "Who can I speak to?" He searched up and down the line of gunmen, still frantically examining their weapons.

"I'm Captain Davis." A voice came from the back row. "Have you jammed our weapons?"

"Yes, we have." Alexander quickly replied. "But we are your friends, not enemies. We want to speak to your leaders about something very important."

Captain Davis eyed Alexander and the others. "Are you carrying weapons?"

Alexander shook his head. "No, we are not." "Then follow me...all of you." He motioned with his hand. Alexander waved to the others to approach. The time travelers followed a small group of soldiers, and went ahead of the larger group. On the street they were directed to load into the back of a jeep. The ride was only ten minutes, to a military outpost.

They were escorted through a door that led to a large office. A distinguished looking officer stood and made his way around a desk. As he approached, a scowl stood out on his face. He crowded to within two inches of Alexander's face. "Who are you, and where did you come from?" His scowl intensified as he finished his sentence.

Alexander had difficulty controlling his temper, but he didn't let it show. He stepped back, looking directly into the officer's eyes. "We are from the future and the past, and we have come to deliver a warning. You have one week to avoid nuclear war."

The officer's eyes bugged out. "I want to know what you've been smoking!" He looked over at his assistant. "I don't have time for nut cases like this! Just send them to General Scott."

The soldiers escorted them into the hallway, and up two flights of stairs. At the top was general Scott's office. From his desk, he motioned for them to come in. Walking over to meet them, he invited them to sit down. The soldiers remained standing, as he pulled up a chair for himself. "OK," he began, "all I'm asking for is an explanation. You see, I have to tell the president and the press how this happened."

He looked from Ed to Kibble to Alexander. "So tell me, why did you land there, and how did you jam all of our weapons?"

Alexander rested his elbows on the table. "I'm going to explain it differently to you than the guy downstairs. You may have trouble believing this, but we are time travelers. We have come to warn you of an event that you can avoid if you will listen to us. This event is nuclear war."

The general lowered his eyebrows and stared at Alexander. "Everyone knows about the saber rattling going on in the international community." He shifted slightly in his chair. "What I need to know is if it's true what you say... the part about time travel. If you want me to believe it, take me for a ride to another time."

Alexander nodded. "Very well. When and where do you want to go?"

The general halfway grinned. "For me that's easy.

1863, at the battle of Gettysburg.

Alexander glanced at Derek, who gave a nod. "We could take you there if you wish." He continued. "We don't have to fly the helicopter. The time machine is inside of it."

General Scott drummed his fingers on the table. "OK," he said, "but tell me a little bit about yourselves first."

Alexander motioned to his companions. "These three are from your own time. Their purpose for time travel is to save their world from nuclear destruction. They traveled back to my time in 323BC to assist in changing history for this purpose."

General Scott interrupted. "So who are you, Alexander the Great?" he chuckled at his own joke.

"Yes, I am." Alexander showed a serious expression. General Scott's smile faded. He turned his palms upward. "OK, I will believe it when I see it. Let's go."

CHAPTER FIFTY-TWO

The group headed back out, this time accompanied by general Scott. Arriving at the white house lawn, he cleared the party for access to the helicopter. He was very skeptical as he stepped into the cockpit, but knew he must go through with this in order to prove the whole thing to be a hoax.

Kibble volunteered to squat between the seats and hang onto them. Everyone was buckled in while Derek programmed the trip. "OK," he called out. "To July 1 of the year 1863, location Gettysburg, Pennsylvania. We'll be arriving just after the battle of Gettysburg."

Kibble leaned forward to general Scott's shoulder. "We probably won't be able to stay long, but it will be enough time to see what you need to see."

Derek flipped the switch, starting the process. General Scott's face bore no expression. The noise continued, followed by shaking, and a loud bang.

The scenery out the window changed dramatically. The white house fence suddenly became a large field, thick with smoke, and intense with the smell of gun powder. Dead bodies were strewn all over the place.

General Scott's eyes bugged out. He became so excited that he tried to stand up without unbuckling his seat belt. With trembling hands, he released the belt. "By George, this is for real!" He just sat and stared, not moving a muscle.

Through the fog, Kibble saw small groups of Union soldiers verifying the dead. For whatever reason, they didn't seem to notice the chopper sitting there.

"We should get back." Kibble glanced at Derek as he spoke.

Derek began entering the return data, but was interrupted by loud banging on the hull.

Alexander looked out his window and saw a large, mean looking soldier rapping at the door with the butt of his rifle.

"Open up!" He yelled. "Get out here or we'll blow you to hell!"

Looking around, Alexander couldn't see more than three soldiers nearby. "Keep programming!" He called to Derek as he opened the door and jumped out. Jaws were hanging in the cockpit, watching Alexander work. Before he touched the ground, his sword was already drawn. The big soldier didn't know what hit him, as the sword handle rammed into his head, knocking him senseless. The two other soldiers raised mussels to Alexander, but their guns went flying with one swing of the sword. Alexander lurched forward as if to attack. The defenseless soldiers sped off like scared rabbits.

Alexander nimbly scampered back and leaped into the chopper. Derek flipped the switch while the door slammed, and the whirring began.

General Scott's mouth still gaped unchecked at the entire scene. He had no clue his seat belt was still unbuckled, but the spinning still commenced at full force.

On the other side, the white house lawn came into view.

When the men had disembarked, general Scott gathered his wits about him. "Gentlemen, we must return to my office for further discussion."

The complexion of things had changed since the first meeting in general Scott's office. The general sat at his desk and wiped his forehead with a hand kerchief.

"General Scott," Alexander said from a chair next to his desk, "nuclear war is going to start in five days, on March 18. We can stop it, but we need the help of your government."

"Certainly, you have my attention." The general agreed. "Would you join me in a meeting with the president?"

Alexander nodded. "The sooner the better."

General Scott picked up the phone and pushed one button. Soon he was speaking with the president. The time travelers heard only one side of the conversation, but still sensed that the president was not going to cooperate. The general did all he could to convince him, but at length just had to hang up. He shook his head, muttering. "That man is an idiot."

"OK," Kibble roused the mood, "this is how it will happen. The Iranians will be first to fire nucs, but we will intercept them. The Russians and Chinese will both fire at us, and everyone will be blown away."

General Scott glared straight ahead. "Well," he looked at Kibble, "what is your suggestion?"

Kibble glanced at Ed, then back to the general. "We don't need the president's approval. This is professor Ed Worth. He invented the weapons shutdown system."

Ed took the initiative. "All I need is two hours on the main computers. I will set up this system via satellite. None of our enemies will be able to fire their nuclear weapons...ever. If they want to attack with conventional weapons, they can try, but we'll shut them down too."

A smile crept across general Scott's face. He slapped the table. "There's no sense in worrying about my job now. We've got to save the world."

CHAPTER FIFTY-THREE

"This is what we'll do first." The general spoke as he stood. "We'll go down to secure the helicopter to a different location. I'll go with you right now." He pointed to Ed. "While we're gone you can start working on the computers." He opened a door next to his desk. "It's all in there." Ed smiled and hastened to begin his all-important task.

At the white house gate there was tighter security than before, but general Scott still managed to get everyone in.

While the four men fastened themselves in, Kibble spoke up. "So General, we need a safe place to park this helicopter. An address will do."

The general took a note pad from his pocket and started writing. "This is my home address." He said. "The back yard is huge and vacant. It's perfect for this." He tore off the note and handed it to Derek, who took only a few seconds to get coordinates from the address, and program the trip.

It wasn't long before everyone heard the boom, and saw the expansive grass of general Scott's back yard. "Fantastic!" The general still did not cease to be amazed. "Now you men can stay in the apartment above the garage. It looks like we're on our own, so I hope your friend can get that system installed."

"He will." Kibble assured him. "Ed will be done within the hour, and he won't need any help. Once the system is up, we should stay here and lay low for a few days. Ed will go ahead and disable all the nucs in Iran, Russia, and China.

Then we'll simply wait for the developments."

"Very good." General Scott unbuckled and opened the door. "I'll take the other car back to the office."

The time travelers hung around the apartment, awaiting news of Ed's project completion. They were delighted that afternoon to see him arrive with general Scott, who stood at the apartment door for a minute to speak with the group. "The situation is getting grave. Everyone is worried, and the military is on high alert."

Glancing at Ed and then back to the others, he continued. "Ed assures me that their weapons are now disabled, but it's still nerve wracking."

Kibble held up one hand. "You saw how the scanners worked today. Well, they work just as well on nuclear weapons. We've proved that in the other time thread."

The general nodded and smiled. "Thanks for the reassurance. I'll talk to you tomorrow."

The next day brought quite a splash to top military brass. Iran complained that their weapons were down, and brashly blamed the U.S. for 'interference'. They threatened swift retaliation. General Scott brought the news to the time travelers during his lunch break. "The entire military, including the president can't understand why the Iranians' weapons are down, even though I have tried to explain this to them. But this is causing them to prepare for war."

"That should not be of any concern to us." Kibble conjectured. "Their weapons are down. We should expect the Russians and Chinese to soon follow suit. They can make all the threats they want, but it won't do them any good."

The next day it happened as predicted. The Russians claimed their weapons were tampered with, and threatened all-out war against America. The Chinese did the same that afternoon.

Ed went to work with General Scott the next day to expand the weapons shutdown system. He viewed satellite photos of all the military installations, and easily used the satellite to guide his scanners and disable everything. He completed the task in one day.

The top U.S. authorities were desperately searching for an explanation for all of this, since they were being blamed for it.

General Scott finally called the president again to re- explain what had happened. This time he got a positive response, and was told to be present at a high-level meeting, and to bring the time travelers with him.

The meeting was scheduled that same day with the president and top officials. They were all seated and eager to get started, as the time travel crew filed in.

Plush carpet and expensive chairs greeted their arrival at the long conference table.

After being seated, they felt many eyes staring at them.

It was as though they were somehow out of place in this world.

The president opened the meeting by addressing the visitors. "Now we have no time for this monkey business. I don't want to hear any time travel nonsense. Who are you people, and where did you come from?"

Alexander glanced at Kibble and Ed. No one seemed anxious to speak, so he took it upon himself. "We are the people who have disabled the weapons of your enemies. You should show more gratitude."

The president was an overweight man in a suit that looked too small. He stuck his fingers into his collar as if to loosen it around his neck. "You speak with an accent. Where are you from?"

Alexander remained motionless, and answered him simply. "Greece."

The president's eyebrows narrowed. "What is your name?"

Alexander pushed his chair back and drew his sword, laying it softly on the table. He sternly looked across at the president as he answered. "My name is Alexander.

Alexander the Great." He viewed those around the table...about 15 people. "I am here with these three men from your own time. We are here to save your world."

The president was speechless. He turned his gaze to the high level officials around him, and then to General Scott. "Is this true, General Scott?" His face had turned red.

The general held out both palms. "Yes, Mr. president. I traveled with them to the battle of Gettysburg. It was real!"

The president bowed his head and cradled his chin in one hand. He addressed Alexander. "So you can really permanently disable their weapons?"

Alexander nodded. He motioned to his left side. "Professor Ed Worth is your man for that."

CHAPTER FIFTY-FOUR

A moment of silence passed, broken by a man sitting next to the president...the secretary of state. "Gentlemen, it seems we are very much in your debt. I, for one, thank you for taking the initiative before nuclear war broke out."

"That's the thing." Kibble jumped in. Nuclear war did break out, world wide. We escaped with the time machine, vowing to somehow change the course of history. We have finally succeeded."

The president shook his head. "This is the most amazing course of events I have ever seen. I really didn't think time travel was possible." He reached up and unbuttoned his shirt at the top, loosening his tie in the same motion. "I don't know where you men are going from here, but I implore you to leave us the scanning technology."

Alexander looked at Ed, who nodded his approval. "Everyone here must decide for themselves, but we all came from a different time thread... same year. We conquered civilization in the same manner. But in that world I am the king of America, so that is where I must return."

"I'll just say this," the president smiled, "that you are all welcome here anytime."

At the conclusion of the meeting, the time travelers spoke informally with the presidential contingent.

Arrangements were made for Ed to teach top scientists about the scanner technology. Alexander and Kibble discussed some details about their travels. Everyone was amazed and fascinated to learn their plight and experiences.

The group eventually ended up back at their guest apartment. Late that afternoon, they were lounging on couches sipping coffee.

Kibble directed a question to Ed. "So how long will it take to brief these scientists on your weapons shutdown system?"

Ed lowered his cup. "To do a good job, I will need two days."

Kibble nodded. "OK, sounds reasonable. Here's what I have in mind. I have no children, and have never been married, but I do have siblings and parents. I would like to take this time to see them and explain time travel to them. I may be able to convince some of them to return with us."

"It's a good idea for you." Ed replied. "As I said before, I have no close family ties, but I do wish you well."

"How about you, Derek?" Kibble continued on point. "Anyone you would like to coax to start a new life?"

Suddenly put on the spot, Derek held his breath and exhaled slowly. He sat his cup down on the table. With a nervous grin, he answered. "I'd like to see my family. I've got parents and a younger brother and sister. It would be great to get them into a good situation like we have in the kingdom."

"I have a tremendous idea." Kibble said as he scooted to the edge of his seat. "We'll time our arrival for just before nuclear warfare. Everyone should be happy to return with us."

"Now that is a sneaky plan." Alexander raised his cup with a smile. "Let me get back to relieve Dennis, and you gentlemen can take as much time as you need."

After a good meal, the time travelers gathered at the chopper. Alexander was dropped off at the kingdom so Derek and Kibble could recruit their relatives. Ed continued the weapons shutdown training, and would be picked up in a day or two.

Three days later the foursome met in Alexander's office, everyone seated in plush chairs around a table. "Well, I am wondering," Alexander began, "if your relatives are now with us."

Kibble chuckled. "I was able to convince my parents that coming with me was preferable to going through nuclear war."

Derek chipped in. "And my whole family was easily convinced in the same way."

"Splendid." Alexander slapped the table. "I will see to it that they all get whatever housing they need." He pulled his chair back and swung one ankle across an upper leg. "Let us just review our progress. I would say we have reached our stated goals, which were to save America from destruction and make it a better, safer place. Of course, we didn't realize we would be crossing time threads, but that has worked out well. I guess I want to ask what you see happening next."

CHAPTER FIFTY-FIVE

"I think you are right." Kibble jumped in. "We have definitely reached our stated goals. As far as what happens next, the answer is simple. We'll know when it happens.

Until it happens, maybe we should just live. Run some tests to make improvements on the doormac."

Derek agreed. "It would be nice to get back to the lab for a while. But I want to make one thing clear. Time travel is now in my blood. It's what I want to do. The excitement and the benefits from it are endless."

"I've got plenty of my own ideas to keep busy." Ed laughed. "Now that I can have as much government funding as I need, I'd like to improve the weapons shutdown system. There are several other beneficial projects that I'd like to delve into."

Alexander leaned back in his chair, hands behind his head. He suddenly broke out in laughter. "Do you know something?" He sat up straight. "All three of you are researchers. "That is what you do. It is your job. My job is to lead this country." He reached down and pulled out his sword, softly resting it on the table with two hands. "I always thought I would live and die as a soldier." He looked at each man. "I now realize that is not who I am. Who I really am is an angel of mercy, an enemy of death."

He held out one arm. "We all are friends of peace.

Icons of time travel. I salute each one of you."

Kibble showed a knowing smile. "You speak the truth.

We are no longer just researchers. We have changed the destiny and improved the lives of millions. Who knows how many we have saved from certain death. We are not just time travelers. Whatever else we do, we will always be linked to the good deeds that changed history for the better."

Derek shook his head and laughed. "I guess this means that we have to always be ready for a trip into the past, or maybe even the future."

"Well, it sounds pretty exciting." Ed grinned. "I'll certainly sign up for that."

Alexander picked up his sword and swiftly slid it back home. "You are all true warriors. Go home and relax, but be ready to come back when the need arises. We are going to run this world the way it should be run. No more wars, violence, crime, or oppression. This is the utopia men have dreamed about over the ages."

When the meeting was over, and everyone had gone home, Alexander stared long and hard through his big window. A smile slowly crept over his face. He had finally done it. He had conquered the entire world. But not just one, but two worlds!

Lightning Source UK Ltd.
Milton Keynes UK
UKHW021848140620
364909UK00002B/212